Dusty's Adventures: The Beginning

by T.J. Akers

Illustrated by Rebecca P. Minor

Author: T.J. Akers

Cover Art: Aponi

Illustrator: Rebecca P. Minor

Editors: Kathrese McKee
                Grace Bridges
Co-Creator: Mark Peterson

Dusty and Mark Peterson may be contacted for visits at www.DustysAdventures.com

To children worldwide:

May you grow up to have healthy and happy lives!

Contents

CHAPTER 1

The Moon Lady, The Wentzel, and Dusty

An unfamiliar smell slithered through my alley near the Pike Street Market, where the yummy fish were sold. The late afternoon Seattle air stung like the prick of a cat's claw as every hair on my tail jumped to attention. Something was about to happen.

This reminded me of something Mama always warned about when I was small, and my brothers and sister were still around. "My lovely ones, if your tail bristles for no reason, run for a tree and climb, or hunker into the tall grass and be still. Weasels are coming."

Too bad there weren't any trees or tall grass around my wooden crate. And Mama was long gone. I depended on the piles of moldy newspapers and thrown-away bottles strewn along the brick walls of my alley to keep me and my home hidden. Sometimes, like right now, I wished I didn't live in the city

Loud scrunching sounds from large claws echoed through the air as a nasty stink wafted toward my crate, flattening my whiskers. This wasn't the possums coming to visit, or the Rottweiler from the deli across the street. A shiver started in my paws and raced up my legs.

The scrape-scrape of strange paws scratching through

the gravel warned that something big was coming, something different.

Hmm, it better be terrible too. Anything that noisy would probably starve otherwise.

Snuffling sounds puffed along my thin wood wall, setting the hairs on my tail on end. For a moment, I thought they'd all pop off. Then the world fell silent.

CRACK!

The walls of my crate exploded into a cloud of splinters as enormous fangs snapped shut within a whisker's width of my face. The stench of rancid breath was suffocating, but at least now I could see what hunted me.

The top of the varmint's head was shaded with grays, whites, and specks of black, like any reasonable animal. But up close, this thing wasn't reasonable. It was multiple shades of weird.

Its forehead was nothing, but bare skull and two empty holes sat where its eyes should have been. Well, not quite empty. A blood-red glow lurked inside them. Its lower jaw and neck were as large and fleshy as the pit bull that lived two blocks east of here, maybe bigger. So that's what Mama was talking about when she mentioned weasels. No wonder she said to hide.

My heart pounded, but not with fear. I should have been terrified, but all I wanted to do was teach the stinky thing a lesson for wrecking my house. This weasel had earned itself a prickly mouthful of claws and a prompt shredding of its underbelly, or my name wasn't Kitten.

The monster got my best hiss. I would have arched my back too if there'd been room, but the smelly thing pushed its face closer still, snarling and snapping its teeth. It pressed me hard against the only wall of my home that was still standing.

A quick duck and scurry put me under its jaw, making enough room to scoot beneath it. All the better to find its soft spots and rake them with my claws.

I thrust my paw upward, claws extended. The tips scraped against a bare, bony spine and fur-covered gristle. The weasel had no belly, soft or otherwise. As for its tail, the long, snaky thing offered more of the same boniness.

"Hey, weasel. What happened to your tail? Get it caught in too many doors?"

"Our master promised us yours when we catch you," it

10

hissed.

The thing folded its body and its head snaked around, trying to draw me into a crushing embrace and rip me to shreds with its back claws.

A sly feint and a quick dodge made enough room to clear its grasp and I shinnied past its bony spine and up toward its face. A fast lunge and my claw hit its target, one of the glowing eye holes.

"Take that!" I shouted.

The weasel jerked away.

"Scram, you mangy monster. Leave that poor cat be." A lady's voice echoed through the early evening air like the ringing of a bell.

The weasel backed away. It trilled and yipped before slinking off into the shadows down the alley.

A set of human hands scooped me up. I yowled and hissed, ready to scratch.

"You are a fighter," she said. "A little black ball of chaos and attitude. You remind me so much of someone I know."

I clawed and bit her hands, good and hard, but it didn't bother her. The lady's warm fingers found their way behind my ears and scratched. So unfair.

For crying out loud, I was purring. Not just my average purr either, but the kind I reserve for special occasions, like finding leftover tuna.

"Hello, Kitten," she said.

Part of me wanted to shred the lady's hand for not minding her cat manners, but the other part never wanted her to quit scratching.

"How do you know my name?"

"A distant family member of yours told me about you."

"My dad? Old Tom?" I leaned my head harder into her fingers.

"No. Someone more like a great-great-uncle or a fifth cousin twice removed. His name is Grimalkin." She grinned. "He does favors for me, and I help him every now and then." The sound of her voice soothed like a good lie-down in the cool earth on a hot day.

"Grimalkin was right," she said. "Wentzels don't frighten you at all."

"Not wentzels," I corrected. "Weasels. We never call them by their proper name. Mama always warned that doing so made them more powerful."

She turned me around and pressed her lips to my muzzle. Her face was narrow and thin, pale as the white surface of an early evening moon.

"Of course," she said, releasing me from her kiss. "My mistake."

"Who are you?" I placed a paw on her nose.

"I'm known as Liosa, but I've gone by many names. Some even call me the Moon Lady, but I allow my friends to call me Lisa." She scratched me under the chin. "Now that I've marked you with my kiss, you are a friend. Whenever you need help, if any other friends of mine are around, they will come to your aid. Unfortunately, it won't be of much help should you come up against Magus."

"What's a Magus?" I squirmed in her hands. She seemed nice enough but allowing a stranger to hold me sent the willies snaking through my tail.

"The master of the thing that hunted you, my darling, but first things first. It's time to get you a new home."

"This is my home, and I like it well enough. Let me go." Her eyes shifted to the pile of sawdust on the ground and then back to me. She lifted her eyebrow and gave me a half-smile.

I wriggled, a little at first, but when her fingers didn't release me, panic set in. I pushed my back claws at her, but every time they found something to dig into, it was like scratching sand.

"My claws are sharp, and my feet are quick and quiet. I'll be fine on my own."

Her grip clamped tighter around my shoulders and rib cage, so I twisted harder swinging my back end in circles trying to reach something vital.

"Oh, Kitten, if you were dealing with ordinary animals there wouldn't be a problem. These are wentzels pursuing you." Lisa paused. "I'm sorry, my mistake again...the weasels have found you. They will be back."

I continued struggling. "Why?"

"Not enough time to tell you, but let this suffice for now, this isn't just about you. There's a lot more at stake."

My breath was nearly gone from fighting, so I stopped and gave her a thick growl while flicking my tail. Hey, I was tired. You go a few rounds with a big, stinky weasel and see how much fight you got left.

"I'm sending you to a ranch," Lisa said. "To be looked after by my friend. His name is Dusty, a big yellow horse as bright as a full moon and as brave a hero as any you will ever meet. He'll keep you safe and look after you. Consider it temporary for now, but if you do this right, you may find a new family with him and the others."

"I already have a family, thank you." I growled some more.

"Of course you do, but one cannot have too much family in this life. I think Dusty will benefit from having you around as well. Ready?"

Her last statement earned a harder flick of my tail and a flattening of my ears. "I don't want to go anywhere. I can handle any weasel that comes my way." I puffed out my fur to look bigger. "My family will come back someday, and I want to be here for them. Don't take me away."

"This is best for all."

My tail swished faster, but the lady only chuckled, making the air around me quiver.

When her laughter stopped, everything went black.

Seattle was gone, and I found myself nestled between two round feet as smooth as river stone but as hard as concrete. Long, strong legs towered high into the air, supporting an enormous mass above me. My gaze followed the shape and revealed a massive body connected to two sets of legs, the ones I stood between, and the other set behind them.

The air here was sweet and warm, nicer than where I'd come from. Something almost as soft as Mama's fur brushed against the top of my head and blew a warm, wet breath over me. It might have been pleasant had it smelled like canned sardines and dead mice, but no, it smelled like grass...clippings.

"Have you ever considered a breath sweetener?" I asked. "Something nice and fishy?"

"Hello," the muzzle said. "My name is Dusty, and you smell like you've just bathed in wentzel spit."

I glanced about and found myself in a corral fenced on all four sides with a small open gate in one corner. On the other side was a wider gate and a gravel driveway. Trees lined the fences and to my back, a good long scamper away, sat a house. The rustle of more big bodies could be

16

heard coming through the small gate. There was also the scratch-scratch of mice and other prey about the place, and the faint scent of...

"You mean weasels." I waited for my tail to bristle. Nothing happened.

"Stay right where you are," Dusty said.

"What if I don't want to?" I flicked my tail in contempt. The horse wailed a terrible racket, sounding as if he were hacking out a fur ball and laughing at the same time. "If you stay between my feet, you will be safe from getting stepped on by the others, not to mention there are things on the prowl tonight. Evil things looking to gobble up little kitty cats." His nostrils swelled as he took in a sniff of air. "Since you smell like one of those things, I bet you're the reason they're here."

I wanted to correct him, but his head bobbed up and down, and within seconds, we were surrounded by two more animals just like him. "This is my sister, Daisy."

A brown horse with soft eyes pressed her nose against me. Memories of Mama flooded through my head, reminding me of the way her rough tongue brushed the sides of my face and the warmth of my brothers and sister

17

cuddling next to me. The new horse whuffled a greeting.

"My sister says you've been kissed by Lisa," Dusty translated.

Another horse pressed his nose toward me and opened his lips as if he were going to eat me.

"Big Red, don't do that." Dusty nudged the horse's head away. "He really won't hurt you. He's curious and insists on tasting things that interest him."

The massive beasts didn't set off my tail like the weasel from earlier. I even flicked it a few times and waited, but it didn't bristle. Still, a faint scent of weasel reached my nostrils.

The sun was long gone, and a less-than-full moon hung in the night sky, surrounded by stars I didn't recognize.

Finally, my tail bristled, and the thumping of my heart quickened. Maybe it would be best to stick with the horse until I figured out exactly where I was.

"Hold on a moment," Dusty said.

The big animal practically tiptoed over me and stood a good length away from the corral's fence line. The other horses fell silent.

A set of glowing red eyes, followed by a flash of

yellowed fangs, peered around Dusty at me. I see very well in the dark, even if the big horse liked to block my view. Hey, I'm a cat.

Dusty snorted and set all four feet in place, as if someone was going to push him backwards and he wasn't going to allow it. Then came a small breeze scented with weasel-stink. It was a combination of window cleaner, human sweat, and rotten eggs. Hmmm, new perfume, Eau de Weasel.

Daisy and Big Red barely breathed as Dusty's ears went flat against his skull. Then the whole night went quiet. Unlike it had in my alley in Seattle.

A flurry of snarls and growls burst through the air in a storm of scary sounds. Dusty let out his share of squeals and then bellowed like a thunderstorm. Two seconds later, weasel feet skittered away in a full out run. The big horse reared up on his hind feet in victory. He made his way back, planted his feet on both sides of me, and stood still.

"You know where those feet have been, right? You going to wash now?" I asked. "They're full of weasel spit."

Dusty laughed.

A new smell wafted in our direction, something slightly different from the smell of horses, similar, but not the same. An animal was nearby, just out of sight. I could hear the clop-clop of smaller hooves coming nearer. The corral we were in was square, but a gate in one corner opened into darkness. This new animal shuffled toward us while the horses paid it no notice. They didn't even flick an ear in its direction.

Then I saw it.

The thing had big, long ears and a much smaller body than the horses.

"That's Jangles." Dusty tossed his head. "He's a burro." I glimpsed red in the burro's eyes, and his gaze made my tail tingle. Jangles flattened his long ears and flashed a set of big, chisel-shaped teeth at me.

Maybe it was me, but I think that burro just hated on me.

Dusty's toasty breath flooded over me. "Lisa told me you'd be coming to stay awhile. Since you brought some unwanted company with you, sleep between my front hooves tonight. It's not safe to wander out beyond the safety of our token. I'll keep you warm and safe from harm."

"How about if I sit on top of you?" I asked. Like all cats I prefer the highest point possible. Aside from a fence post, Dusty was the tallest thing out here.

"No." Dusty wagged his head from side to side. "Stay where I can keep a closer eye on you. The token, our moonstone, keeps all the nasty things of the night from coming past the fence and onto the property."

I like prowling new places, usually, but here, the smells were strange, and I felt small and afraid. I hunkered down between the horse's hooves and flicked my tail. "You mentioned a token, and a moonstone. What's a moonstone?"

"My human friend Mark and I have adventures hunting what he calls monsters. Sometimes, things follow us home. It's the moonstone, a gift from Lisa, that keeps our home safe. Like tonight, something followed you, but it couldn't come in."

"I wasn't afraid, and if you had let it come in, I would have taken care of business," I said. "I beat up a weasel just like it earlier today."

"A what?" Dusty asked.

"A big gob of teeth, bone, gristle and...something."

"A wentzel," Dusty said. "You meant to say wentzel."

"Yeah, that's what I said. Weasel."

Dusty trumpeted a big sneeze through his nose toward the fence. "I doubt you defeated a wentzel but have it your way. You need to understand that not caring about anyone does not make you fearless, it makes you lonely. Loving those around you so much that you would do anything to keep them safe, that's what gives you courage. Funny thing is that you feel all kinds of fear at the thought of losing those important to you. The more people in your life you love, the more there is at stake, and the more you feel."

"It sounds tedious," I said.

"I'm not surprised you feel that way, but you're young and have a lot to learn."

The breeze shifted and now floated in from the north. I sniffed, and the memory of the weasel from earlier stirred fresh in my memory.

"On second thought, the trip here was taxing." I yawned. "Wherever here is. A bit of sleep does sound good." I closed my eyes.

Grass Bag seemed pleasant enough, but he sure was bossy...and smelly. At least his breath was warm. It flowed over my head and neck, making my eyelids feel heavy— even if it did smell like lawn clippings. The rest of the horses didn't fan out. They grouped around me and the big yellow guy.

Dusty yawned. "You'll meet my friend Mark in a little while, when he brings breakfast. You can stay for now, since Lisa sent you, but to stay longer requires Mark's approval. After all, he has to feed you."

A soft weasel trill echoed in the night air setting the hairs of my tail on end. The big guy pushed his nose down toward me.

CHAPTER 2

In Tuna I Trust, But Only a Little

Sleep during the middle of the night? Not my thing. Cats live to prowl in the dark, especially me, but every time I tried to sneak away, the old Grass Bag had to cramp my style. You know...Dirty, Muddy, or whatever he called himself. He'd give me a snort of warm, moist breath, and I'd go straight back to sleep. Like his breath was magic, or something.

Before I knew it, the sun was popping up and a human-shaped shadow bobbed about the grounds. Yep. I drew in a long sniff. A human. There goes the neighborhood.

Daisy and Jangles rubbed their heads against the human and made soft, rumbly noises in their throats.

It seems horses and burros purr too, who would have thought it? Marking your property made perfect sense to me if there were new creatures around, but the way these horses perked up their ears and tapped their feet against the ground made me think they really liked this human. They even meowed to him.

Well, not really meowed. A horse's call is shrill like someone whistling and coughing at the same time. It's so...annoying. The burro's call was worse. Jangles squeaked and honked like a wounded goose with its beak caught in a trash can lid.

As for the human? He carried grass for the horses, which was admirable. If these animals had a human serving them, maybe they weren't as dumb as they looked.

Myself, I've never cared for humans. The fact that their movable thumbs makes them useful is irrefutable, but you can't trust them. Still, Grass Bag remained calm and peaceful as the human shuffled along. Daisy followed the human closer as Big Red pressed harder into the huddle. They were like a family.

"Dusty?" The human peered in our direction. The man ambled about, wearing a funny hat. His voice sounded as if he laughed easy and probably never yelled, at least not a lot.

"Dusty? What's the matter?" His shoulders slumped, and his voice gained a tinny edge. He seemed honestly hurt that Dusty didn't go over and mark him the way the others did.

"That's Mark," Dusty whispered to me. "He's my friend. You will be polite to him. If he likes you, you can stay. If Mark doesn't like you, you must leave. I'm sure Lisa also told you that being here means following my rules."

"Can hearing your rules wait until after breakfast?" My stomach growled as ferociously as a pack of weasels.

Dusty snorted. "You're pretty sure that there will be an 'after breakfast.'"

The human carried one last hay bag slung over his shoulder as he staggered toward us.

"Dusty! No wonder you didn't move." Mark set the hay down. "You have a new friend." The man bent down but stopped short of touching me. At least he didn't grab me like that Lisa. This man gave me space.

"Aren't you cute?" he asked.

Well, of course I'm cute. Goes without saying. He needed to be more specific if he was going to get on my good side.

"Your black fur and yellow eyes will make you the perfect Halloween decoration." Mark's head tilted. "Your coat is all matted as if you've been slobbered on. What a mess. Maybe you'd like something to eat? Then we'll clean you up."

Well I wanted to take a bath, but every time I moved, Dusty started breathing on me. I flicked my tail, waiting for a warning of danger. This human didn't puff it out one bit.

Let's see how bright Mark was. I tucked low and held my tail against the ground while offering a growl. Nothing mean, more like clearing my throat to be noticed. I didn't want him thinking I could be taken for granted.

"That's okay," he said. "You can stay there for the moment." Mark reached up and stroked Dusty's cheek. "You've been watching out for this fur ball all night?"

Fur ball? He just called me a fur ball!

Dusty rumbled a deep, throaty purr from his throat as Mark stepped beneath Grass Bag's chin to accept a hug. The big yellow goof seemed to really like this human. Stranger yet, the human liked Dusty back.

I tried a human once, but all he did was throw things at me. Sometimes he fed me, but most of the time he kicked at me or threw me outdoors without feeding me. Humans were despicable creatures. Trust them, and they'll toss you to the weasels the moment you turn your tail to them. I've questioned the very existence of humans capable of caring. But just for moment, a twinkle of an idea warmed me. I wonder what it felt like to have a human who wouldn't hurt you?

"Little guy," Mark said. "If you want to eat, you better follow." Mark turned and walked away. "The house is up this way."

"You heard him. Get moving," Dusty whispered. "Oh, and don't forget rule number two."

"Was there a rule number one?" I stood and crooked the end of my tail in a question mark.

"We don't let the humans know we can talk, let alone understand them back. Keep all communications simple, alright?"

I flicked my tail. "Meow."

"Rule number one, we get along. We don't hunt, hurt or injure one another on this ranch. This is a safe place. Got that?"

"Meow."

"Come on, Kitten," Mark muttered. "Can't you hear the tuna calling?"

I allowed the tip of my tail to curl in a most satisfying loop. I shouldn't be thinking with my stomach right now. Dad always said, "If your whiskers get cramped going someplace, it's best not go to there. Always think with your whiskers." Dusty may have had rules, but so did I.

My rule number one? Depend only on myself, unless tuna was being offered. Even then, only trust in tuna a little bit.

As I followed Mark, there came an unpleasant jabbering from the other side of the fence. It was half growl and half whimper. "I'm coming for your tail, Kitten. You can't hide from us or our master."

I stopped and took a good long sniff. It was only a noise, but my heart beat faster.

"Coming?" Mark asked.

I risked a glance behind me. Dusty flattened his ears against his skull and let out a big, horsey growl. The big yellow horse stood like one of those stone statues near my home. If he'd been on a pedestal he couldn't have looked more fearless. His whole being appeared as if he was challenging the world to cross the fence and get zapped with his magic moonstone. I do need to teach him to start calling them weasels instead of wentzels.

The Big Guy wagged his head from side to side and pawed the ground twice. The jabbering faded, and the human wandered about his business as if he were deaf and blind to everything that just happened. Maybe Mark wasn't so clever after all, or maybe the moonstone did— stuff. There's something going on at this place for sure, but no matter what, this big yellow horse hadn't seemed to be anyone's fool.

CHAPTER 3

When Weasels Fly

I stepped off the porch of Mark's house and made my way in the direction of the corral and pasture gate. I couldn't believe I'd slept most of the day in this new place. Well okay, maybe I could. Tuna always made me sleepy after eating. It was because of this morning I realized why Dusty kept Mark around. The human was useful, thumbs and all.

Out in the pasture, the full warmth of the afternoon sun stroked my coat and tail. It felt good. Then again, most things felt good when my belly was full. Something nagged at my tail. It wasn't tingling yet, but it felt like it wanted to. Time to saunter a bit and get the lay of the place.

"Hello, Kitten," a voice called out from behind me. The big guy appeared from nowhere.

Startled, I ran for the nearest tree, but Dusty grabbed my tail and didn't let go. At least he had the good manners not to bite down.

I reeled around to smack him, but he released me before my claws found their mark. I tumbled backwards and barrel rolled to a standing position. It took a moment to calm my heart. Suddenly every hair stood to attention and remained standing on end.

"Why, I ought to—"

"Ought to what?" Dusty's ears pricked forward, and his brown eyes were earnest and...likable.

"How'd you sneak up on me?" I asked. "That's hard to do, especially for someone as big as you."

"I have my talents, but you're the one that's really mysterious," Dusty said.

"Oh?"

He bobbed his head. "For one, you like to call wentzels weasels, and they don't seem to scare you. You know what happened out here earlier, right?"

With a small sniff, I gazed here and there. There were downed trees and broken branches scattered everywhere. Nearby, parts of the pasture fence had been flattened by fallen tree trunks. Daisy, Big Red, and Jangles were nowhere to be seen.

"The place looks like weasels ransacked it," I said.

"And that doesn't bother you?" Dusty asked.

"Should it?" I asked.

"Lisa sent you here because something known as Magus is after you." His soft, brown eyes made me feel welcome.

"I don't even know what a Magus is. It's not like I've ever seen one."

"I only know the stories my mother told me when I was a colt. She said Magus was once a magnificent creature, bright and powerful as the morning sunlight. One day, he went mad and turned on the whole world. He likes to cause all kinds of problems."

A mid-summer breeze swept by us. Dusty turned and pricked his ears up, his gaze turning dark as he peered out toward the open pasture.

I flicked my tail at the Grass Bag. "Sounds like the kind of story your Ma tells you at bedtime."

"Weren't you the one calling wentzels some other name because your mother said so?"

"And we've both seen and smelled the stinky things too. They even drooled on both of us, proving my Ma was right." I stretched. "One good whiff of you and I can't say there's even a hint of Magus spit on you. Not that I know what a Magus smells like, but hey, this is all new to me."

Dusty snorted at me. "And yet you met Lisa. If there's one, why not others? Mother said Magus wasn't the only one of his kind. There was a battle between them. They managed to kick him out of their herd."

"So, Magus sends weasels to eat innocent kittens, and little...you called yourself a horse, right? To eat kittens and horses. I think Lisa did mention Magus now that you mention it."

Dusty nodded and then bobbed his nose in the direction of a fallen tree. "They're not beings to be taken lightly. Look how those birches over there were snapped like twigs."

I drew closer to a cluster of fallen tree trunks that littered the ground.

"What do you make of that?" Dusty asked, following.

"The trees are freshly downed," I said. "When I arrived, they were standing. I can see deep, evenly-spaced grooves in the tree trunk and the stump. They're like the traces I leave when my claws rake across telephone poles and other things."

Dusty grinned. "Go on, what else?"

"The big difference? Those marks were made by bigger claws than mine." Images of the weasel from yesterday poured back into my mind. "It doesn't look like they stepped onto the pasture."

Dusty nodded. "If wentzels set foot on this side of the fence, our moonstone, or token, dissolves them. It would be best for you to stay in the house, but if you must go outside, stay away from the fence lines. Wentzels like to knock trees over and use them to get deeper into the pasture." A big grin spread across his face and a mischievous note entered his voice. "Until someone knocks them off and they hit the ground."

I raised a paw and licked it, then paused. "Is that what happened here today?"

Dusty watched a passing bird for a moment and appeared to forget my question. "Did you notice the moonstone when you were in the house?" Dusty asked. "It's a big stone with squiggles on it. Mark keeps it inside."

"I don't remember. There was a lot of brushing and the tuna distracted me," I said. "Using a tree to reach you is really stupid. What about your human? Do they ever go after him? Where is he, anyway?"

"He was in town when they showed up," Dusty said. "Wentzels seldom bother us. Now that you're here, I wonder if that might change. What did you do to Magus to make him mad?"

"No clue, I never met the thing in my life. Has Mark ever seen a weasel?"

"Wentzel," Dusty replied.

"You shouldn't use their true name," I said. "Their name fuels their power and creates more fear. Calling them weasels makes them weaker, and a lot less scary."

Dusty snorted. "The stone not only hides us from the Magus, it also hides a lot of things from humans too. Lisa prefers as little human interaction as possible. If Mark had been here, the stone would probably make the weasels appear as a storm. It would be up to me to protect him though." He paused, pricked his ears up and stared at the far end of the pasture. "If you're going to be out here, at least stay close to us in the pasture. It's not good for you to be by yourself right now. There's probably more wentzels around."

"Weeeeaseeeels." I blinked at him and flicked my tail. "I know what I'm doing." It was like talking to a telephone post. "See ya later."

Dusty snorted again, flashed me a look, and trotted off.

What can I say? I'm a cat. I don't do what I'm told. A quick scamper and leap put me on an old stump near the broken tree that flattened a section of the fence. I arched my back to work out the kinks.

I'm sure Grass Bag wondered how I managed to sleep through such a commotion, and with all the downed branches and trees, there had been a lot of commotion out here. It would be prudent to panic, but a belly full of tuna makes it hard to panic or wake up from a sound sleep. Even so, this kind of mess should have had me up in an instant. Dusty said something about the stone being inside. Maybe it made me oversleep.

I muttered to myself. "When I go back in, I'm going to look for this so-called moonstone. It's probably some cheap souvenir like what the tourists throw at me down by the fish market."

A big round cat-face popped out of thin air in front of my nose. "The moonstone is a token, given by my kind to their chosen heroes. It allows its bearer to draw upon their patron's powers and abilities. No direct connections anymore, safer for everyone involved."

I didn't jump, hiss, or twitch. The sun filled me with

calm and peace. Apparently, weird no longer scared me, but it probably should have. "Moonstones, token, yada, yada."

The face grinned and blinked.

The good news? My tail didn't puff out. The bad news? This silliness apparently is my new normal.

"Buzz off," I yowled. "This is my stump, and this is *me* time." I straightened my back and wrapped my tail around my feet.

"The polite thing to do," the face said, "would be to say, 'Thank you for having Lisa bring me here.' Then you should introduce yourself. My name is Grimalkin. And you are?"

"Manners? Of course, manners would mean you giving me a better explanation of why I'm here, if you have one. My name is pronounced best as KITT-en."

"Of course, you're KITT-en, Sonny Jim. Now, do you want the long version of your predicament or the short one?" Grimalkin's gray body appeared as he crowded next to me on the stump. He was about twice my size. His eyes glowed green, and that strange grin of his was getting creepy.

"Don't call me Sonny Jim. If you've got answers, spill."

"Lisa would probably be the one to speak with, but she's not much of a day person, except certain times when the moon is out along with the sun. She's better at night and early mornings." Grimalkin sighed. "Worse yet, the poor dear is just not herself these days. I heard you ran into a weasel yesterday."

I paused. "You called them weasels, like me. Why?"

Grimalkin purred. "All my kits have learned that a creature's power is bound in its name. Make light of the name, and it siphons power from the fiercest of things."

"I like mispronouncing wentzel more for the fun of it." I flicked my tail.

"Well, there's that too." Grimalkin examined the claws on his right front paw. "I'm here because you're going to need some intervention."

"What's that?" I asked. "And why do I need it?"

"Intervention is offering you help just in the nick of time. As for why?" Grimalkin purred a low, rumbly purr that I was sure made the stump shake beneath us.

"So, trouble is coming and you're purring?" I asked.

The fact that this weirdo nutcase was purring in the

face of oncoming trouble was disturbing to say the least.

"In about three seconds or so, a burro is going to be dashing across the pasture in this direction. It will be chased by flying weasels."

"Wait, flying?" I glanced around.

"Yes."

Jangle's honking and braying vibrated over the pasture. I couldn't see him, but he was easy to hear.

"All of you Lisa-types are positively annoying, popping out of nowhere and spoiling my activities." It was important to flick my tail for emphasis. "You also didn't make my tail puff out. What am I supposed to make of that?"

"Lisa-types?" He chuckled. "We are what we are and follow our own council. In case you're curious, in about twenty seconds, the burro is about to become roadkill."

Jangles came loping into view.

"There's no road there, how can he be roadkill?"

Three black weasels, the size of poodles, flew into view like a flock of swallows. They had skull faces and big claws. They also had wings like bats. Just for a moment, all the fur along my backbone and tail stood up.

"Okay, I can see why you might use the term roadkill."

"You going to just sit there, Boyo, or you gonna help?"

I remembered Mama's words. You didn't start the fight, you shouldn't interfere.

"True." Grimalkin yawned. "I used to think that way too."

"Hey, did you read my mind?"

"Sort of. But the best reason to help is because the big yellow horse needs someone to watch his back, and this would be a good time to prove yourself. You're here for more than just your protection." Grimalkin blinked at me. "You're not the only one, Boyo, in need of help in this world. Sometimes you have to give help to get it." The giant gray cat raised eyebrows and yawned. "You have only a few seconds to decide if you're part of the problem or part of the solution."

"They're chasing Jangles. What's that got to do with..."

A queasy sensation fished around my gut. Something was wrong with this picture of Jangles and flying weasels, other than the weasels were as ugly as bald gerbils, and twice as unnatural. There was something else I couldn't quite put my paw on.

"Dusty'll be charging over here any minute to answer Jangles's plea for help," Grimalkin added. "The big fella is most attached to that burro."

I watched Jangles for a few more seconds. The burro circled in a very specific pattern, moving parallel to the barn, but never going any farther away or moving closer. When I'm chased, I head straight for cover, or a high place. Why didn't the burro run to the barn? There were no fences to stop him and the corral gate was open.

Jangles ran harder in the shape of a big oval, his small feet pumping as hard as they could. When the weasels flew at him, he would dart in their direction and scoot beneath them. Once under them, he could have darted for cover, but he didn't.

Instead, he started the pattern all over again.

"I can hear the wheels in your head churning. You're catching on," Grimalkin said.

The burro repeated the oval once again. I moved closer to get a better look at the flying weasels. They were the strangest looking things I'd ever seen.

"Is this a trap?" I asked, looking back towards the

stump. "Is Jangles working for Magus? It looks like Jangles is setting Dusty up."

Grimalkin gave a long, slow blink, but didn't answer. "I can't take out the weasels for you. That would be against the rules. However, should you decide to be part of the solution, I can tell you that all you must do is jump on top of them and drive them to the ground. The minute they hit the grass, Lisa's token does all the hard work."

"That sounds like a lot of effort to me. Lisa's token? You mean the moonstone?"

Grimalkin nodded and went silent, but I could think of no reason why he would lie. Still, it never hurt to be cautious. There's definitely something wrong with everything here.

"What if I think you're lying?" I looked back at Grimalkin.

"Now you're starting to sound like kin of mine." Grimalkin flicked its tail. "You don't know what to do? Trust your tail. If you want some help, I'm happy to budge Jangles closer. Can't do more than that, there are rules to be followed."

My tail stayed normal. "Who writes these rules and

where can I find them?" I glanced at the burro and then back at this strange cat and sighed. "I'll do it."

"Being part of the solution, and not the problem. Good for you. Just remember, make sure to jump above the weasels and not directly into their claws." His body faded, leaving only his head in sight. "Get ready, Sonny Jim."

"Well, duh. And my name is Kitten. KITT-en"

Grimalkin's head shrank to a black speck the size of a small stone. It launched itself toward the burro and hit him in the flank. Jangles kicked and bucked, changing direction in the process and moving closer toward me. The weasels hovered in the air, paused, and altered their flight paths.

The black speck flew once again into Jangles's flank, making the burro lunge into the air. With each new leap, Jangles edged closer to me. The wide-eyed look of bewilderment on the burro's face filled me with more questions, but those would have to wait for later.

Jangles ran several more patterns, and each time the black spot struck his flank, the burro changed course. He eventually moved close enough for me to touch him as one of the weasels followed. It changed direction and dove at me. My tail puffed out.

Wait, I wasn't supposed to be the prey.

I crouched beneath its swoop, measured the distance in my head as it circled around. When the weasel swooped toward me, I was ready.

After one exceedingly fine leap, I found myself above the weasel with my claws buried in its gristly shoulders. It dropped like a rock and smacked into the ground. On impact, the weasel went up in a putrid-smelling vapor.

I was going to need a bath after this.

Since us cats land on our feet, I was none the worse for wear, especially because a weasel cushioned my fall. Old Grimey was apparently right about getting rid of these things.

The burro raced by again. This time he grazed the fur along my back with a well-timed kick.

"Hey, that was on purpose! I'm on your side, stupid." But he gave me an idea.

The burro repeated his pattern, but this time I was going to cut him off, scramble up his shoulder like I was climbing a tree and rush on to his back toward his butt.

The burro retraced his steps back in my direction, and

off I went. In seconds, I had scrambled up his shoulder and onto his back. He gave a stout buck as I dashed across his back bone and sent me flying high into the air just as a weasel passed beneath me. I came down on top of the thing, all claws drawn. The second weasel and I plummeted to the ground.

"Weasel Burgers!" I yowled as it went up in in cloud of stink.

Dusty let out a bellow from somewhere deep in the pasture. The faint rumble of his hooves grew closer. I wasn't sure how fast he'd arrive.

As the vapor cleared, I looked up. A big set of claws bore down towards my face. "Oh snap, I've been suckered."

"Looks like Magus is making them smarter these days," Grimalkin hollered from the stump. "I'll make a note to myself."

"Make a note, right." I rolled my eyes.

Before those sharp, talon-like points found their way into my face, a well-placed hoof connected with the weasel a whisker's breath above my nose. The thing careened out to the other side of the pasture and into the brush.

"Three points," Dusty whickered.

"What?" I asked. "What's three points?"

"I don't know, Mark always says it when he throws things at the garbage can from far away." Dusty stood by me, breathing heavily and sweating. He stared down at me with that stupid horsey grin as Jangles barked like a dog chasing a car. Wait. The burro was barking like a dog?

Jangles came to a stop near us and had the nerve to give me a look that screamed, "Are you nuts? I had everything under control."

Dusty snorted an answer in return. "Kitten did what we're all supposed to do, look after one another. Getting along keeps the moonstone working for the times Lisa can't help us. But what I saw of you, Kitten, was impressive. Maybe you did defeat a wentzel yesterday."

Dusty's grin didn't mock or make fun of me. He pressed his nose to the top of my head and roughed up my fur.

"Yeah." I yawned. "I guess rule number one doesn't apply to weasels, right?"

The burro gave me a beady-eyed stare.

"Thank you, Kitten," Dusty said. "If they had gotten

Jangles, we would all have been devastated."

"Wait, backup a minute. What did you mean when you said, 'the times Lisa can't help us?'" I asked.

"Lisa's power comes from the moon. She's strongest when the moon is full, which doesn't always help in the daylight. When the moon isn't full, it might be up during the daytime, but she doesn't have as much power as she used to. She's also ancient and we think she's showing her age. We guardians eventually pass on too."

"So, she's not all powerful?" I yawned. Weasel fighting really drained my tuna energy.

"Powerful enough, when she needs to be." Dusty swished his tail.

Jangles moved toward us.

I yawned big and wide, couldn't help it. "How about a ride back to the house? I'll mind the claws."

The big yellow horse walked to my stump and allowed me to get on him.

My neck hairs prickled under a strange but an easy touch. A collar tightened until it fit just right. A small object dangled from it. It tingled against my chest, but it was hard to see.

Gulp.

I'd never worn a collar before. When I glanced at the stump, Grimalkin's face appeared against the bark and gave me a long slow wink.

"My gift to you," he whispered. I pawed at it and it wriggled, but the strap was well fitted and didn't budge.

"Many of us on this ranch have our talents," Dusty said. "Daisy has a few. Jangles does too. He mimics all kinds of sounds."

"Do they all talk like you? I don't understand them very well, especially Jangles."

"No, they only speak like normal animals, but Kitten, you've got skills too. You can understand them and can make them understand you. If you're anything like me, the more time you spend around other animals, the easier it becomes to communicate."

It had never occurred to me that most animals couldn't communicate outside their own kind. I always thought everyone could understand everyone. Well, except humans. Humans don't even understand one another.

"Lisa said something about Magus wanting me. Why is that? I never heard of him until yesterday."

"Dusty, Daisy, Jangles, Red. Where is everyone?" The voice was human, but softer and higher than Mark's. It belonged to a girl, and she was walking in our direction. "Are you okay? Come here."

It took quite a few minutes to get back to the corral. Somehow, I hadn't remembered it being so far away.

There near the wide gate stood a human, someone that wasn't Mark.

CHAPTER 4

Meeting Kenzie

It's Kenzie," Dusty whispered. "She lives next door and takes care of us when Mark has to go away."

Grass Bag whiffled back a sound that was a cross between hacking a fur ball and snickering. It nearly made me fall off him.

"Cat, mind your claws," Dusty snorted.

Dusty made another shrill calling noise and started toward the girl. The rest of the horses appeared from out of nowhere and fell in line behind him.

A truck trailed up the long, graveled driveway toward the house and stopped. Mark got out. "What happened?" He pushed his hat back off the top of his head as his gaze scoped out all the fallen trees. "I saw trees knocked down all along the north side of the pasture fence."

"I think a storm cell came through," Kenzie answered. "This will take me a day or two to clean up for sure." "Who is that magnificent black cat on Dusty?" Kenzie walked closer to meet us. "He's beautiful and looks so cuddly."

"I think he likes to be called Kitten, or KITT-en. At least he answers to that so far. I tried a bunch of different names and he acted like I wasn't even in the room. When

I told him, he was one stubborn kitten, that got a purr out of him. So, Kitten is his name. Let me introduce you."

Mark was learning after all. Good manners are so important. He got a nice long squint from me.

The girl stepped right up to Dusty. She was slim with long dark hair that curled at the ends. Clearly, she wasn't Mark's offspring. She looked nothing like him. Most importantly, she called me beautiful and cuddly. Smart girl, definitely not related to Mark.

Dusty dropped his hip and let me slide to the ground. Before I could dig my claws in, I found myself in Kenzie's arms, and she was...petting me.

"My name is Kenzie, and you have to be the most precious thing in the whole world." She didn't crush me in her grip but held me just firmly enough that a wiggle would set me free in a flick of my whisker. Then she said the magic words. "You're too skinny."

What a remarkable human. Yes, I was too skinny. This girl was brilliant.

"Not to worry," Mark said. "There's cat food in the truck. And treats."

Personally, I was hoping for more of that amazing

tuna. It was good for this cat's soul.

"Kenzie, why don't you take Kitten inside the house while I put the horses and Jangles in the barn. I need to take a good look at all the fences before I let them out again."

Kenzie scratched behind my ears. "Mark, I got my learner's permit yesterday. You going to let me drive your truck?" She glanced at the house and set me down. "Don't answer. Let me get Kitten taken care of, and then I'll come back and help you clean up. You can let me drive then."

"Don't hurry on my account," Mark said. "Maybe you can convince Kitten to stay with us."

Kenzie smiled at me. "What do you say, Kitten?"

I grinned at Grass Bag, holding my chin high and pushing my chest out. Do you think Dusty grimaced or scowled like a sore loser? No, he took all the fun out of my gloating by smiling the biggest, dumbest grin I'd ever seen. He looked pleased with himself as if he had planned everything.

I flicked my tail, telling him, "Just you wait, Grass Bag."

Kenzie set me on a table next to a big rock. I didn't remember seeing it last night, but I'd paid little attention to anything other than tuna. Besides, I lived in a wood crate, who was I to judge if someone put a rock inside their home? She walked away, but as she did, my tail began to tingle.

I gave the rock a good sniff. I'm curious by nature, so I took a closer sniff.

"You sit there, um...Muffin?" She tilted her head at me. Oh no, you did not just call me Muffin. Dude! Muffin?

Seriously? I liked the name Kitten. KITT-en.

"Do you like the rock? It came with Dusty when Mark brought him home. It was part of the deal. Daisy came the next year, but he didn't get another rock. The rock must always stay on the property Dusty lives on. It was in the bill of sale." She picked up the bag of cat food and a heavenly scent rolled off the paper cover. It smelled a lot like the fish market from home. "There was also something about it being protected in the bill of sale. If it broke, or got damaged, Dusty and Daisy had to be returned. Weird, huh? Mark figures it should be safe there."

Kenzie left the room with the bag, but she made lots of noise wherever she was. For a minute, I was tempted to follow, but decided to be lazy for a moment longer and see if she would come back with some in a bowl.

I sniffed the rock again, pawing at the shapes and symbols cut into its surface. Every time my nose or paw touched the symbols, the stone buzzed like a bee. It smelled like Lisa the Moon Lady too. This must be the moonstone that Dusty was talking about.

Kenzie came back and set a bowl on the table. It was full of little stick shapes that smelled like tuna. Time to eat. I could check the rock out later.

One sniff of the bowl, and I meowed.

"Don't tell me you're going to be Mr. Finicky now."

I flicked my tail.

"Oh, right. You need a litter box."

Grass Bag was right—I can make other animals understand.

CHAPTER 5

Trouble

The days and weeks passed quickly. There had been no more weasels and life on the ranch had become...acceptable.

The house was dark, my tummy was full, and the warm mid-summer night beckoned me through the open windows.

"Kitten," it said. "Come out and prowl."

The evenings in this new place had interesting sounds.

There was the warbling of birds I'd never heard before, but since Grass Bag had rules about hunting on the property, I wasn't able to sample any of them—yet. All I could do was listen to the new sounds along with and the soft wheezing chirps from something Dusty called cicadas. My favorite was the constant pitter-patter of scurrying rodent feet out in the yard. My mouth watered just thinking about it.

But tonight, my ears caught a small twitchy gait belonging to something completely different. The sound was soft, but not beyond my ability to hear.

What caught my attention was the odd scraping sound that made me think it must be a four-legged creature with a fake leg. It made a pad, pad, pad, thump-scrape. Okay, I admit, the whole scenario sounded like one of those bad television shows Mark liked watching

It sure wasn't the rabbits from last night, or the pack rats living in the burrow at the north edge of the ranch. This was someone, or something, out of the ordinary.

Then the sound came right up to my kitty door, stopped, and then whatever creature made such a commotion scrambled away in a fury of padding, thumping, and scraping.

What? Who would dare come to my front door without permission? There was no way this side of the litter box I was letting this go uninspected. I raced out my kitty door and into the night.

In between the chirp of the cicadas and the grumpy croaking of toads arguing over turf, a different sound burbled out from the summer warmth. I couldn't quite put my tail on the sound, but I was going to find out the owner of that sound or my name wasn't Kitten.

I stalked toward the hay shed that sat next to the driveway entrance. A soft scratch-scratch-thump against the outside of the hay shed drifted toward me on a fresh breeze. I gave a quick sniff and a listen. There was nothing new or unusual, only the continued scratch-scratch from the shed.

The noise made me think of moderate-sized claws, nothing large mind you. More along the lines of a baby muskrat, or maybe a plain old rat. I was off to investigate. Grass Bag hadn't talked about a rule against tormenting intruders before running them off. At least if he did, I hadn't heard him. Ignorance, in this case, will be bliss.

Each step closer made the sound grow softer. Maybe I shouldn't bother and go back to bed...naaah.

"Probably two sets of claws scratching," I said softly.

To be on the safe side, I went the long way around. This meant going by the grain bins behind the shed. After all, there was no reason to be careless. Grass Bag was always going on about the moonstone keeping the evil things out, so I supposed that must include all the normal creatures that were less than friendly. I checked my tail. Nothing.

I rounded the bins and scanned the area in front of the shed door. Whatever made that noise was nowhere to be seen, but I heard something from inside the shed.

This was no longer interesting, we have now officially

reached the point of homicidally annoyed. The nerve of some stranger coming to my kitty door unannounced, and then not introduce himself before running off. That was rude. Someone was going to need a lesson in cat manners.

This called for one last check of my tail. Nope, still nothing evil here. Then I stalked forward to the shed entrance and peered in.

The hay shed was my second most favorite place on the ranch. My first was my kitty bed. The shed was appropriately dusty and full of spider webs, stinky mouse droppings, and thousands of hidey-holes, burrows, and other fun places to investigate. It never got old or boring. One day I found a garden snake and properly chased it out. This was my turf and I knew every hiding place to climb into, except for the new one that now appeared beneath the hay bales. Yep, a brand-new, never- explored hidey-hole. Life kept getting better.

Even in the dark, I couldn't miss the enormous corridor beneath the great stack of hay bales. It was always fun to try to get between the spaces Mark created as he stacked bales. Most of the time he shooed me away with a good scolding.

"Don't you get in there," Mark would say. "You're liable to get stuck. You've gotten fatter since you first arrived. We can't have you getting crushed if something causes the bales to shift."

Phooey with that.

Tonight, there was a brand-new, Kitten-sized tunnel tempting me from dead center at the bottom of the stack. Since Mark wasn't around to shoo me away. I was in it as fast as Dusty gobbles grain.

The old dust smelled of hundreds of unique things that tickled my nose and made me sneeze, good and hard. There were so many fresh traces of mice under here that I was sure I'd hit the jackpot. Maybe even snack on one or two—Grass Bag would never find out. Then came the sound of tiny feet scurrying out the other end, followed by a voice I didn't recognize.

"Hey, what happened to the thing with the gimpy leg?"

"Very astute on your part," a squeaky voice answered. "But I must admit that getting you here was easier than all of us thought."

The voice was high-pitched and resonated crisply through the crevices where bales didn't press against one another.

"Now that you are completely under the whole stack, you might get yourself crushed."

Definitely a mouse.

The hay bales above me tilted and shook as the inner bales shifted, causing my passageway to narrow. That was my cue to leave.

"Oopsey," the mouse voice squeaked.

A quick wiggle and I headed for the opening in the back. I hadn't gotten more than a good scramble toward it when it disappeared, along with every other opening big enough for me to wiggle through. A cloud of dust showered over the top of me, revealing the awful truth. I was stuck. My body was wedged so tight, even my tail couldn't move.

"It wasn't you that did that, was it?" I asked.

A tiny "tee-hee" from a different voice tumbled downward from the bales above my head. "Oh, the great cat is now stuck. Heeee-heee. Best of all, no one is around to hear you call for help. The horses are at the far end of the pasture tonight, and Mark is asleep. So yowl and holler, kitty cat, be as loud as you want. No one will hear you."

"Okay, who are you, and what happened to the other voice?"

Silence. No one answered.

Not being one to give up, I wiggled, hard. Guess what? I still couldn't move. When my tail tried to flick, it couldn't move either. Worst of all, it didn't fluff out. Here I was in danger, and all it would do is keep its usual, elegant form. My toes tingled, but the tingling didn't stop there. It kept creeping higher up my legs. I needed to move. Worst of all, I was going to have to cry for help.

"Meeeeooooooooow," I called. "Meeeeeeeooooooowr."

No one answered.

"Meeeooooooooow," I repeated. "Meeeeeooooowr."

"You sound pathetic," squeaked a third mouse voice above my head.

"Come closer to my teeth and say that, Squeaky."

"Now, now," the first voice spoke. "Let's be pleasant. Our intention wasn't to harm you. We just wanted to make an introduction. A type of introduction that would impress you at the same time. Besides, you aren't in any position to threaten, cat, but since you seem to have everything under control—we'll leave you to it."

"Www-ait," I said.

"No, no. You're right. Everything is under control," the third voice laughed. "But not your control."

This was embarrassing. Mark just put extra bales up close to the corral and wouldn't be down here for several days. Sure, I could call and maybe he might hear me, but then again, it could be a while. Grass Bag would probably come looking for me, once he noticed I wasn't around. That wouldn't happen until tomorrow afternoon. I could manage the wait if the bales didn't move any further.

"I don't know why you're bothering me," I said. "I've kept the rules and left you mice alone. Besides, even if you wanted to help me, mouse, you're not big enough. You don't have enough hands and movable thumbs strong enough to move the hay."

"We didn't need them to put you here," it answered back. "We don't need them to get you out. Besides, we'll tell Dusty. He'll do the rest."

"Tell Dusty?"

As if being stuck here by mice wasn't embarrassing enough. The big yellow horse would be doing the rescuing, that was if my snack-sized captors passed the info. Knowing the Grass Bag, the big guy would probably never let me live this down. I don't know what worried me more, my tail not puffing out or that the mice did this without magic. Hmm, I guess I'm confused about what my tail is telling me. Am I in danger, or not?

"You went to a lot of trouble on my account," I said. "You made your introduction; my name is Kitten. What do you want now?"

"Not much, not really," the second mouse said. "We also wanted to show you that we aren't helpless against you, or anyone. We would make better allies than enemies."

"Aaaandddd?" I asked. "Just who are you?"

"I don't know if we should say right now," the third mouse answered back. "Besides, who we are isn't as important as what's happening on the ranch. How about we let you out and you owe us a favor?"

"I'll owe you?" I snorted. "Ha!"

"I'm sorry," the third mouse said. "I didn't hear that."

A quick look around was enough proof to convince me to agree to their demands but being put in this place by things normally eaten was disconcerting. "Fine, I'll owe you," I said. "You got me."

"Fair enough. We will send word to Dusty," the mice spoke together. "After you promise."

"I did. Who are you again?" I asked.

"You'll remember us with no problem. Your word, out loud and no tail flicking."

"As if," I mumbled. "We heard that."

"And you didn't hear me give you my word?"

Silence, no one spoke.

"Fine," I said. "Again, my word."

No one answered.

"Soon we will have information for you. Things you need to know...and as a courtesy, we won't tell anyone that it was mice that trapped you."

"How kind of you," I sneered.

"One last thing," they said in unison,

"What's that?"

"Watch out for the burro."

It didn't take a genius to figure that out, but then again, not taking things seriously on this ranch can get a cat into a lot of trouble.

"Hey, before you go, I really wanted to ask you something...it's important."

No one answered. The silence extended into long minutes, then I heard heavy footsteps beyond my prison.

Several bales to my right shifted and wiggled, causing a tunnel to open and filling the cramped space with night air. I scrambled to freedom past Dusty's huge, questioning face. "I'll explain later," I called over my shoulder as I hurtled toward the house.

Lisa was so wrong about this place. The mice here were almost as bad as weasels. How did they get the bales to trap me?

The early morning sun blanketed my back and tail with delicious warmth. Normally, I'd be delighted with a sun bath, considering I was nearly crushed by a bunch of hay bales in the dark hours of the morning. Then there was the matter of the mice getting heavy hay bales to shift.

Right now, I felt more like hiding than sleeping. I didn't want to deal with Dusty teasing me about last night. Answers were still important, but they probably weren't coming from Dusty or Grimalkin. My favorite stump in the pasture beckoned.

The weasels did me a favor knocking over that tree. It was near an old stump that was properly cut down. Without that jagged mess, I would never have found it. No jagged edges for KITT-en's little behind. Besides, the spot was the perfect place to keep an eye on the horses, and Jangles, with the least amount of effort. On the plus side, the brush beyond the fence was thick and would make it hard for anything trying to sneak up on me.

Everyone munched on pasture grass as if they didn't have a care in the world. Daisy lifted her head up and scanned the pasture before returning to her snack. That was when an enormous shadow darted across the pasture. My tail wigged out. In a twitch of a whisker, I scrambled to the ground and pressed myself against the stump. What in the name of tuna was going to grab me now? I braced myself, and...nothing happened.

From my new hiding place below the stump, I surveyed the pasture a second time, much more cautiously. The shadow passed, and the daylight came back.

Boy, I was getting jumpy, but can you blame me? For all that hooey Lisa said about being in a safe place, the ranch was proving to be anything but safe. The shadow disappeared, and I took my place back on the stump.

This time the silhouette of a large bird hovered over the pasture. Not a single horse moved, flinched, or looked up. It was as if everything was normal.

A ginormous black silhouette soared through the blue sky above the horses. Normally, shadows move across the ground, not through the sky like this. It wasn't a bird, it was the shadow of a bird with no bird to cast it, as wide as Dusty was long. Then there was the hair on my tail starting to stand to attention.

Normal bird? Normal, my tail.

I'd made a living hunting, especially birds. I know the difference between a shadow and a bird.

Dusty hollered at me from across the pasture, but he was talking with his mouth full. I assumed he was telling me to get home, but the distance between us made it tough to hear what he said. His Horsiness needed to get his rump over here and give me a ride to the house—wait, strike that. He should come over and let me walk under him while he sheltered me from air attacks. This was a pasture after all, and there was no cover. I certainly didn't wish to become anyone's fast food pickup.

"Shh," one of the squeaky voices from last night said. Then came the sound of that funny three-legged gait followed by a tiny wooden thump. "Follow me."

I looked down and nearly fell off my stump. A small brownish lump of fur, with big ears and beady black eyes peered up at me from the ground. I knew it was the three-legged mouse. I'd recognize the sound of that limp anywhere.

I liked my lips and swallowed. "You know, it's really rude not to introduce yourself."

"Cat, I don't have time for this," the mouse answered. "There's something going down at a spot on the other side of this fence, and you need to see it. Once I set foot off the property with you, I'm mouse waffles. Dusty's rules, right?"

I nodded.

"Promise me safe passage from this spot and back, and I will show you something you need to see."

Safe passage? Of course not. The little morsel was

right about his being safe on this side of the pasture fence, but all bets were off once we stepped over the property line. Fortunately for him, I wasn't hungry. So, I pretended to look the other direction while using my nose to size the little goober up.

"Not interested." I flicked my tail.

"Magus is having a chat with Jangles."

I looked away. "It's none of my business."

"Oh, you're not still mad about last night."

"The burro is eating out in the pasture...." I sighed.

"It only looks that way. Magus is pulling a magical fast one on everybody."

"What about the moonstone?" I asked.

"If Magus doesn't touch the ground, he's fine. But even he can't fool your tail." The mouse twitched his nose and my tail frizzed out as if it was a bad hair day. "You have questions? I have answers. Truce?"

When did mice start ordering me around? Great barking dogs, first my tail poofs out at the first sign of only-fate-knows-what, then a bunch of mice get the drop on me, and now a mouse wants me to stroll with it where who-knows what could be waiting for me. I flicked my tail.

"Cat, I don't have all day."

"Deal. You do know there's a huge bird out hunting right now?"

"Did it puff your tail out?" the mouse asked.

"Duh." I brought my tail around to the show the idiot.

"Good, stay under the cover of the trees. Oh, and for the sake of cheddar, be quiet."

My eyes followed the little brown mouse ball bouncing about the place until it stopped.

"Lead on, Squeaky."

He darted from beneath a sumac branch and headed for an oak. He then scrambled up the trunk. I followed.

"Impressive." I paused and gathered in a better look at the mouse. "The three-legged rodent has mad skills."

"Get a move on," the mouse said. "We don't have all day."

"Where we going?" I asked.

"Not far from here there's a clear spot with an old rotten stump. The burro will speak into it and talk with Magus."

"So that wasn't Jangles in the pasture, it was magic?"

Squeaky paused, looked over his shoulder and made a *tsking* sound. "Rookies. Keep your yap shut. You'll hear the burro for sure, but you can't always hear Magus screaming back, you have to be quiet for that."

"Oh, goody," I said.

Finding Jangles didn't take long. In fact, he stood in the middle of a clearing just like the three-legged mouse said. He peered down into a big, black lump of wood. The whole place reeked of sour milk, like the carton Mark threw away yesterday. The whole business puffed my tail even more. I was sure anything to do with Magus always smelled this bad.

The burro spoke into the mass of rotten wood. "You promised, you gave your word."

You could have knocked me off the branch. Jangles's voice was soft and low, but not raspy, unlike when he brays. His voice even sounded pleasant.

"I thought he was...."

"Shhh," the mouse hissed.

Jangles was a good distance from our tree, but I could hear him just fine. What I couldn't hear was if there was a voice talking back.

"Stay here," Squeaky whispered. "Don't move. I need to hear what Magus is saying."

The little brown morsel disappeared through the brush without a noise, squawk, or even a scrape. He impressed me, but if anyone repeats this to the rodent, I will deny everything.

The burro stood motionless for a while. The sun was past its crest and moving toward the afternoon.

Jangles's long gray ears drooped lower with each passing minute. His head fell and he tucked his tail as if he were bracing himself for a beating.

"You promised," he said again.

"Come on, cat." Squeaky reappeared. "What?"

"Shhhh, freeze," the mouse hissed.

The burro's ears pricked up as his gaze moved around the clearing.

A cold feeling snaked in my gut, and for some reason, I thought Magus was ready to pop out of the stump.

"Don't move," Squeaky whispered. "Just wait."

The burro stared in my direction for a bit, then went back to peering into the moldy mass of rotted wood.

"Go back to the house," Squeaky said. "You're safest

inside the house with the token."

"What did you find out?"

"Not now, we'll be heard. Come to the barn after dark, you need to hear what Magus said."

Afternoon came and went while I napped inside. Once I got up to prowl, it was time to find out what the mouse heard.

I headed for the north gate, up by the barn, when my nose picked up a ticklish smell. It was part mouse...and part something else.

The scent lingered from inside the barn door. It was hard to pin down the smell, but one thing was sure, I needed to check this out.

On my way through the door, I stumbled over three dead mice. That strange smell was all over them. Ick. I'd need to be desperate and starving before those bodies found their way into my mouth. Besides, my belly was still full.

"Whaaaaaaaaaaaaaaaaaaa." Jangles blasted the air with his imitation of a fire truck. The racket sent me up a rafter and scrambling for cover.

Jangles appeared out of nowhere and sneered at me. A hint of red glowed in his eyes. Was it my imagination, or was the burro snickering? I scowled back.

"Hey, stupid burro, why'd you kill them?"

"What's all this?" Dusty poked his head into the barn from

the corral.

"Ahoooooga. Ahoooooga." The burro stood above the tiny carcasses and carried on as if there was a full weasel attack. That was when I noticed one of the mice only had three legs.

"Hush, Jangles," Dusty scolded.

Jangles went silent as Dusty made his way to where the burro stood guard above the dead mice.

Dusty sniffed at the bodies and snorted. "Oh no! What happened?"

I thought about keeping my yap shut, but one of the dead mice was Squeaky. Since the mice were dead, and I was a known killing machine when it came to rodents and small birds, it was easy to see where this was going.

"Hey, Dusty," I said.

Dusty and I were getting along since the flying weasel incident. He was like that obnoxious older brother I wished I'd never had, the one that always bossed you around. But when his gaze traveled from the dead mice to me, his eyes turned moist and weepy. His lips puckered into a little pout.

Jangles let out a series of honks and bellows. And the language!

"He says you did this, Kitten." Dusty's eyes were half-closed and his ears drooped.

"Do what? I just got here."

Jangles snorted.

"Jangles accused you of breaking Rule One."

"I haven't hunted anything since Mark started feeding me. And those are pretty serious accusations from someone I saved from flying weasels."

Jangles pawed the ground and snorted.

"I'm sure there's a good reason why they're here." Dusty nudged Jangles with his nose. "They smell strange...and there's no blood or injuries. Mark sometimes puts out traps and poisons for them. The mice are expected to mind the poison themselves. Maybe..."

Jangles brayed and pawed the ground again.

Of all the nerve! That burro called me an ungrateful, backstabbing liar and that's just the words I can use in front of children. Dusty was right—I was getting the hang of understanding Jangles. The burro was such a potty-mouth, too.

"Jangles, we don't accuse family without..."

Wait. Did I hear that right? Dusty called me family?

The burro lifted his nose and blasted the air with squawking and honking.

"Keep it up, Mr. Potty Mouth," I said. "You may wind up munching on soap yet."

Dusty squinted up at me and whinnied. "Kitten, would you mind hanging out at the house for a couple of days? Jangles wants this whole thing investigated. He's being most difficult. Do it for me, please."

I really wanted to know what the three-legged mouse had found out, but it was too late.

"If I must." Why did Dusty have to be such an old bossy- boots?

CHAPTER 6

The Mouse Committee

Banished to the house? Me? I flung myself onto my bed. Who did Dusty think he was?

Kenzie and Mark sauntered in. She set a pair of gloves on the table. "Thanks for letting me drive the old beater truck. When do I get a chance at the Ram pickup?"

Mark pushed back the cowboy hat on his head. The way his smile flattened, the answer was probably never.

"Let's first get the hang of not-almost-running-me-over-in-the-pasture." Mark grinned. "Granted, automatic transmissions can be a little tricky—you just have to remember to hold the brake down before you shift into drive."

Mark disappeared into the kitchen, and Kenzie tapped her fingers on the tabletop. That was my cue for an ear scratching. I was on the table in seconds.

Kenzie ran her hand down my back and massaged my head. After a moment, she called after Mark. "You asked me about taking care of Big Red, Kitten, and Jangles for you while you're gone on your next job. I don't know if I'll be able to now."

"Okay," Mark called back. "Got something planned? Summer vacation has been going on for a while. I thought for sure you'd be looking for things to do."

Kenzie stroked my head as I plopped down on the table and exposed my belly. "I asked my folks if I could go visit my cousin in Fort Smith, Arkansas. We used to spend a lot of our summers together. She's going into the military soon."

I leaned my head harder into her hand. She always knew exactly where to scratch.

"I wanted to see her one last summer before she left. My folks had a cow when I asked permission. They said no, but I'm not ready to give up." Kenzie's throat was tight and her voice sounded higher than usual. She was sad.

"Plane ticket too expensive?" Mark popped his head out of the kitchen.

"No, I've saved up. It won't cost them anything, but they didn't like the idea of me going on a plane by myself. I'm fifteen and a half, and they still think I'm a little kid."

"Can't one of them go with you?" Mark asked.

"They can't get off work until December, and my cousin leaves for basic training at the end of August." The corners of Kenzie's mouth drooped. "I want to leave my options open, in case they change their mind."

"Mroow." I pressed my front paw against her wrist and purred. There's nothing like a little bit of me to make Kenzie feel better.

"No problem," Mark disappeared into kitchen. "I have someone else I can ask. Let me fix you something to eat before you head home. We got a lot of fences repaired today. Oh, and you need to call your mom to let her know you're still here."

"Parents are a pain." Kenzie leaned over me and wrapped her arms around me, but not for long. She released me almost right away.

This girl was a fast learner and understood me well. I touched my nose against hers.

"I earned the money from you to buy my ticket, fair and square. It won't cost them anything. I still can't believe they said no."

Her hand stroked my neck and ears. I admit, as far as people went, Kenzie and Mark were tolerable. Okay, I liked them. There, I said it.

"Parents are human too." Mark set dishes on the table. "They sometimes struggle accepting the fact their children are growing up." He grinned at us. "I think Kitten would let you drive his truck if he had one."

Kenzie rubbed my chin. "Where's your photo shoot?"

"Southeastern Oklahoma, the Kiamichi Mountains. Dusty, Daisy, and I are leading an expedition looking for Bigfoot." He returned to the kitchen for another load of stuff.

Kenzie laughed. "Seriously?"

"Well, I'll be setting up trail cameras for the people that hired me. Do a little tracking and maybe wrangle up a bear or two for background footage."

"Wait, Oklahoma? Fort Smith would be on your way."

Kenzie quit petting me.

"I know." Mark poked his head out from the kitchen and grinned. "Your folks already spoke with me about it. I'm giving you a ride to your aunt's house."

"Wait. Seriously?"

A large smile stretched across her face. My magic was already working. Kitten to the rescue.

"I don't know what to say. When do we leave?"

Yep, there's nothing like a little bit of Kitten to cheer a body up. Kenzie hugged me again. I leaned into her and allowed it.

"We'll have to get things firmed up here in the next couple of weeks," Mark said. "I'll let you know."

"Hey, you! Cat!" a voice squeaked.

I rolled over on my bed. It was dark, and normally, I would be prowling. But house arrest and a lot of ear scratching by Kenzie had messed with my internal clock.

"Great, voices are speaking to me from thin air now."

Two more voices squeaked in unison. "We came to warn you."

Opening my eyes was a waste of time. My nose told me everything I needed to know—mice. I thought they might want to play pin-the-tail-on-the-cat because their friends were dead and decided I was responsible. Easy to take care of, but then I could hear Dusty's voice in my head, "Rule Number One."

"Go away, I've been banished to the house. It wasn't me that killed your friends."

"We know," one of the mice said. "We have a deal for you."

One of my eyes slipped open and I shifted myself to the edge of the bed. A group of three mice stood in front of me: a fat one, a scrawny one, and a tall one.

"I only hunt when I'm hungry, I eat what I kill, and I never kill more than what I eat. I've kept my promise to Dusty not to hunt you on the property. Now, go away."

"We believe you," the tall one squeaked. "But everyone on the ranch is in danger, us included."

I lifted my head up. "Dusty said something about poison. Shouldn't you be paying better attention to how things are supposed to smell?"

"It wasn't regular poison. We know to avoid that. It was Jangles that killed them."

My eyes flew open.

"Normally, we keep to ourselves. It's safer that way," the scrawny one chimed in. "You haven't hunted us once since you arrived or hunted beyond the fence. It's made us curious."

Got to give these guys credit—they were observant. They also didn't seem to be afraid of me. Maybe I should fix that. I lifted a front paw and started washing it, making sure to spread my claws wide.

"We saw how you fought for Dusty and saved Jangles. You may be a cat, but we think you got honor. You're the perfect sidekick for the big guy."

I yawned, making sure the mice could see all my teeth.

"What's a sidekick? It doesn't sound very nice."

"Well, we watch classic television at Kenzie's house," the scrawny mouse piped up. "One hero we like has a sidekick named after a robin. The robin is always helping the hero out. There's another show about a woman named Lucy, she's got someone named Ethel for a sidekick, she makes all kinds of jokes. Then there's a guy who dresses in green. His sidekick can take out a room full of toughs all by himself."

I yawned. "You don't seem to pay much attention to the Grass Bag. A few dead mice turn up, and I'm under house arrest. That doesn't say much for me as a sidekick, or for your judgement."

"Doesn't matter what Dusty thinks. You have honor," the scrawny mouse squeaked. "You keep your word."

"You said that already."

Come to think of it, the mice were right. I followed all of Dusty's rules, so far. Okay, Barely. Look what it got me—, house arrest.

"It was the burro that killed the mice today," said the fat mouse. "He's not going to stop killing us until he gets you kicked off the ranch and allows Magus on the property."

"How can he do that? I thought the token kept Magus out." The scrawny mouse plopped his rump on the floor and slicked back his whiskers. "One, Jangles is jealous of you and mad at Dusty. Breaking the token is easy. All that has to happen is for everyone to stop getting along." "And you all know this because...?"

All three of them turned their beady little eyes on me and crossed their arms.

"Okay, fine. Let's say you're right."

"We think Jangles fancied himself Dusty's sidekick. We've followed him after the first week you got here. Every so often he'd disappear. We assigned our best agent to him."

"The mouse with the wooden leg?" I asked.

"Yes," the fat one spoke up. "Jangles has been meeting

with Magus every other night since you showed up. Our intel had Magus telling him how to set up the weasel episode in the pasture, and there's the bit about causing you all to fight amongst yourselves."

"You're sure?" I asked. "This sounds..."

"Like a bad TV show," the scrawny mouse said. "We heard about the conversation Jangles had today with the big jerk too."

"Who, Dusty?" I asked.

"No, the other big jerk, Magus."

I had to admit I was starting to like these guys, but it was tough to see these guys as something more than just food. Cats getting personally involved with their own snack is never good.

"Our agent had yet to fill us in on what he heard from Magus earlier today. We know it had Jangles upset."

The scrawny one interrupted. "Our investigators determined the victims died of fright. Jangles had some sort of weed in his mouth that when combined with burro spit intensified their fear."

"I don't think Jangles is all that frightening," I yawned again.

"One of our inspectors believe the suspect imitated your voice too. Made the mice think you and the wentzels were working together."

"He did? Jangles? I have to say you bunch are pretty wimpy if a threat from me makes your heart stop."

"Cat, do we look scared of you right this minute?"

"Well, no."

"We have more to fear if you leave." The tall one stepped toward me. "Having you on the property and not hunting us means we're safe from you and can live in peace. It's not easy when you're low on the food chain."

I supposed that was correct.

"Why don't you go tell this to the big guy? I'm stuck in the house until further notice."

"There's more," the tall mouse said. "We overheard Magus talking to his wentzels last night. He said you weren't the main target anymore. Once the moonstone is taken care of, there's bigger fish to fry. Dusty and Daisy will be easy pickings if all his plans go right."

Could my life get any weirder? My favorite snack in the whole world was telling me I was being framed by a burro that could mimic just about any animal sound he wanted.

Said burro was working with Magus to end me, who may have now changed his mind. I'd never met Magus in my life. What did he have against cute kitty cats? I stood up, stretched and stepped off my bed.

"What do you need me to do?"

"You have to make the deal first," the fat mouse said.

"I already have one with Dusty."

"You have to make the deal with us. Promise to never hunt or eat another mouse. In return, we will become your eyes and ears from here on out." The mice stepped closer.

"We also promise to share everything we already know."

"I see pretty good myself, and my hearing is sharp..."

"You didn't hear what Magus said today, did you?

"Well." I flicked my tail. "What did Squeaky overhear?"

"Promise us first," they said in unison.

"First things first, if you want me to continue to listen, you cannot call wentzels anything but weasels from now on."

"Why?" the fat one asked.

"Too long to explain. Yes, or no?"

"Fine," the tall one said.

"If your services are as good as you say, you have a deal, but only for as long as I live here. Our deal doesn't include chipmunks or anything else." I stretched again. "But first, I want proof that your info is good. Tell me everything."

The three mice huddled and the little guys argued for several minutes.

The fat one waddled forward. He seemed to be the leader. "We'll do even better. Jangles will be meeting with Magus shortly. Understand, if Magus succeeds and Jangles manages to break that stone, Dusty and Daisy have to leave here. There's no one here to protect anyone. Without Dusty, Daisy, and the stone, life will go back to the way it used to be here for us."

"Old information, mousie. Not to mention that I'm still restricted to the house."

The fat mouse sat on his haunches and spread his front paws. "We listen in on everything from Mark's snoring to Jangles's late-night talks with Magus. If you follow the burro tonight, you can catch him in the act for yourself. Dusty will have to believe you then."

"You knew Jangles was a traitor and didn't say

anything to Dusty." I grabbed the fat one with my paws and dangled him by the tail. "I really ought to eat at least one of you."

"We try not to get involved," the fat mouse squeaked. "When you're at the bottom of the food chain, keeping to yourself often means living another day."

The other two cringed, but they didn't run. Brave little suckers, I'd give them that.

"Don't forget, we're exterminated by humans too," the scrawny one said. "Besides, we're mice, no one believes us anyway. We think Dusty will believe you eventually, so we decided to help you prove your innocence. You gonna eat us for helping you?"

I hate it when my snacks made sense. "On principle alone I ought to eat you for not sharing about Jangles."

"Lisa left something with us to give to you, just in case. We're not going to give it to you if all you're going to do is eat us. Eat us now, and we take the secret to our graves, or your stomach."

I glared at the mice for several long seconds. They had me. Maybe it would be better to have them as friends, they had trapped me in the hay bales after all. I set the fat one down. "We'll do this on a trial basis. I swear off eating and hunting all mice for now. In exchange, you work for me, but I'm going to add one stipulation."

"Beside the weasel thing?" the scrawny one asked.

"Yes. You do what I say, when I say, and the big guy doesn't hear one word about our arrangement."

"That's two," the mice chorused.

"Is it a deal?"

"Yes!" they all said.

"Jangles is meeting Magus at the rotted stump fairly soon," the fat one said.

"If what you got isn't from Lisa, I will hunt you all and eat you immediately."

"That's not very sporting," the tall one said.

"Okay, would you feel better if I gave you a count of three first?"

"You're wasting time," the mice squeaked in unison.

CHAPTER 7

The Waning Moon

The moon was waning. Well, you could also say that the moon was done being full for the month. That's what happened when you hung around Lisa-types, or guardians, as Grimalkin called them. You picked up their lingo.

Even if the moon wasn't completely full, it was still bright enough to spot Jangles as he made his way to the gate. I could have gone right to the meeting place, but Dusty isn't going to like straight accusations. I needed to follow his every footstep to gather proof and evidence, if the mice were to be believed.

The burro tiptoed along the back side of the barn near the old tire swing, where I hid in the shadows. The mice might be right about Jangles, but Dusty needed more proof.

Jangles kept his knees bent as he picked up his hooves all dainty and sneaky-like. The burro hardly made a sound.

If he is working for Magus, like the mice said, you can bet I won't go all dainty on his big-eared self.

I'd told Dusty weeks ago, after the pasture incident, that Jangles was in cahoots with the weasels. The burro tried to lure him into a trap that day, or maybe me. Probably the both of us. "Jangles is family," Dusty told me. "He wouldn't do that.

We never accuse family, not without a lot of proof."

Yeah, look at where that got me. House arrest. The big yellow horse was far too trusting. Me? Not so much. None of us could afford that luxury anymore. I needed to prove once and for all the burro was a two-bit, back-stabbing scoundrel, and a traitor.

The burro rubber-lipped the metal doohickey on the north gate and the springy-thing near the hinges shut the gate behind him with a gentle thud. Then he faded into the sumac without a sound.

I scooted under and passed beneath all the tangle and mess. Easy enough, but keeping sight of him might be another matter. I still didn't understand why Jangles would frame me. I never did anything to him. A freezing sensation from my new collar spread across my chest and neck. I couldn't see it, but I felt it. Not sure what that was about since my tail was skinny and calm—for now.

Jangles's feet crunched with each step as he passed over old branches and twigs. He probably felt no one was around to hear him, so he could relax. Hah!

A quick scramble up a tree, and I caught sight of the brush wagging and waving in the burro's wake. Then all went quiet, except for the chirping of the cicadas.

The tree next to me had a long branch that reached over to my perch. In the tick of a whisker I was across and into the next tree.

One branch led to another, and before I knew it, I was passing from tree to tree and keeping up with Jangles. Old forests are wonderful.

The brush beneath me rustled and waved as Jangles moved, but after a few minutes, the trail of tree branches ran out as I reached a gap I could not cross. I was stuck. So much for old forests.

It was important to keep the burro in sight, which meant climbing down and following on the ground. I searched the ground for a spot to land but met Dusty's gaze instead. Talk about a shock.

My tail didn't puff out, but the rest of my fur did. My ears slapped back against my head. "Dude! You can't sneak up on me like that."

He flopped and fluttered his ears to signal "Quiet."

Like he needed to tell me that—I practically invented silent stalking.

Dusty sighed and walked off in the direction Jangles went. He stopped after several steps, turned, and bobbed his head. I was supposed to follow.

"Do you have to be so bossy?"

He snorted, turned, and walked on. Down the tree I scampered. This was a good thing. Dusty would be there when we caught Jangles in the act. No more house arrest.

A few steps later, the air pressed hard on my back and face. There was a heavy, stinging cold to it that even made Dusty wince.

The first time I met a weasel, the air was like the prick of a cat's claw, sharp and icy. This air was like one hundred cats raking their claws across my face and chest. My tail puffed instantly. The sparkly on my collar set to buzzing like a bee. Then the air shimmered around me and a grayish bubble formed around the big guy and me. We were instantly warmed.

So much for stealth. Even a blind weasel couldn't miss us now, but Dusty didn't stop. He glanced at me and winked as he flashed his big horsey grin.

"I didn't do this on purpose. I think it was the sparkly on my collar," I whispered. "Maybe we should go back."

"This is protective magic, like what the moonstone does for us. But it's not Lisa or the stone doing this, is it?"

"No," I said. "It's this collar. I'll tell you later."

The yellow horse nodded and we walked on until Dusty slowed. We were near the place I caught Jangles talking to the stump. A great darkness, as thick as mud, filled the open area. Not a bit of moonlight seemed able to pierce the stuff. We stopped short of walking into it, and my tail puffed out harder.

"Let's press on," Dusty signed with his ears. "I'm sure your trinket would probably let us pass, but we need to move cautiously. Only ears and tails for speaking."

"You sure my trinket works that way?" my tail signed back. This gift for communication was pretty handy.

I don't think it's later yet," he answered with a flick of his ears.

Two more steps and a great cloud of sadness fell on me, as if all the tuna had been drained from the world and was replaced with turnips. That had to be Magus's doing. Attacking defenseless tuna? The creep had no shame.

We moved along the edge of the open space, keeping well beneath the cover of the trees. Good thing my night vision was decent.

The thing on my collar swiveled around and practically pulled me along. If only Grimalkin had told me what the collar was supposed to do. The bauble was okay, but the wiggling and the cold against my neck was annoying.

The outline from a cluster of dwarfed and twisted oaks appeared near the center of the clearing. Next to them floated a shadowy blob, even darker than the night. It looked for all the world like a big greasy stain. Jangles let out a long, mournful bray.

In response, the thick darkness that filled the clearing pulled itself together into one single shape which grew three times bigger than Dusty. It sprouted two legs, two arms, a head, a neck, maybe feet, and a single glowing red spot where an eye might be.

So this was Magus. The moron who disrupted my life and wrecked my home. It was hard to know just what to feel. Anger, rage, contempt, terror, laughter at his lack of style?

"Hail, Magus." The burro squeaked. He sounded

exactly like a mouse. Usually Jangles made all kinds of noises. The burro's ears drooped and he tried to look at Dusty without meeting gazes. I looked up at Dusty, but Grass Bag didn't seem surprised. His brown eye softened and his head drooped a little.

Dusty glanced back and wiggled a response with his ears.

"Right," I flicked my tail. "Later."

A black tentacle poked out from the middle of the shadow form and slivered off a chunk of black from what may have been a leg. It plunked to the ground with a squish. Who knew what he was doing, I didn't. My tail was sticking straight up and the hair stood so straight and stiff, maybe the only thing left would be for it to fall off.

"Burro," the shadow said. "You did manage to bring me the cat after all...and the horse. I guess you aren't a total failure. Pity I've changed my mind about keeping you around."

The burro's ears perked up and he turned in our direction. "Why? I did everything you said." Jangles stepped back. "You're still going to leave Dusty, Red, Daisy, and Mark alone? The cat is all yours."

"Wait." I flicked my tail in a flurry of comments. "The burro is about to bite the big one and he's asking about you and everyone else?"

"It would seem he was concerned about everyone...except you." Dusty dropped his head and sighed. His big eyes were practically dripping tears, but he looked on. .

Even in the dark I could tell Dusty was sad, by the way his ears drooped and his head sagged as he watched on.

"I don't know why you're broken up," I signaled to Dusty. "It would seem I'm the one Jangles was selling out.

The blob of shadow quivered as it let out a low belching laugh. "No. My new plan not only rids me of Liosa, but gives me the chance for unlimited power. The cat and the horses have become irrelevant."

"You d-d-don't need to..." the burro stuttered.

"Harm them? Of course I do, burro. I am Magus. Harming things is who I am and what I do." The blob quivered with more laughter as the temperature of the night dropped even lower.

This Magus wasn't like a person, or anything I'd seen. Even Lisa and Grimalkin were more creature-ish than this collection of shadow and spit. But one thing to be said of Magus, being around him felt like dreaming a big spider was crawling up your neck, only to have it follow you out of your dreams once you woke up.

"The good news, burro," Magus wheezed. "My investment in you was not a complete waste of effort. Especially since I can start by harming the moon horse's sister once the token is dealt with. I believe Daisy is what they call her."

Dusty winced. His ears twitched, and he shifted his weight from right to left. The big guy didn't like Magus threatening his sister.

Magus's shadowy form expanded and a tentacle with a cluster of thorny spines on the end shot out from its center. It seized Jangles around the middle and the burro let out a long, lonely gasp as his ears went limp. The pointed spines dug deep into his body, but they didn't seem to make holes or cause Jangles to bleed. Judging from the burro's reaction, they still hurt—a lot. I might not have liked the burro, but even he didn't deserve this, no one did.

"Little burro, this is where you come in handy." Magus

hoisted Jangles into the air with his tentacle and drove him into the shadowy dark center of his form. "Time to feed."

Jangles fought and kicked. He bit at the shadowed parts he could reach, but Magus pressed the burro deeper into his inky black body until all you could see was Jangles's nose.

Dusty squealed and charged Magus, nearly stepping on me. A second tentacle pushed forward from Magus and took a swipe at Dusty. It knocked the horse into a heap, but Dusty was back on his feet in seconds. Magus pushed the burro's body deeper until Jangles disappeared.

The burro's screams could be heard despite being pushed in Magus' body. I couldn't bear to listen anymore.

Dusty's body took on the glow of a rising moon. He charged the big shadow again, dodging a tentacle, and raced by Magus. With a quick kick from his rear leg, he clipped the inky darkness with a hoof. The shadow cried out. Dusty skidded to a halt, wheeled back around on his haunches, and struck at Magus again with his front hooves.

Magus yanked the burro's body from his form and

threw it on the ground. In the wink of an eye, he drew in upon himself and disappeared into a single spot of black, leaving the glob of shadow shivering on the ground next to Jangles. Dusty reared to stomp the black spot, but before the big guy could nail it, the blob shot off into the brush with surprising speed.

"Kitten," Dusty called. "Stay with Jangles. I'm going after that thing before it reaches the ranch."

Strangely enough, I did as old Grass Bag said. Me, doing what I was told? Somehow, obeying him didn't seem so strange after what we just witnessed.

I trotted toward Jangles and lay next to his head, sniffing and licking his cheek. Poor Jangles. His limbs and shoulders were misshapen as if something had knotted him like a rag, untied him, and left him in a rumpled heap on the ground. I pressed closer against the burro's chest and purred.

A warm pair of hands stroked my head, and Kenzie's familiar voice greeted me. "You were here all night? Mark! Jangles and Kitten are over here."

Mark's normal smile had been replaced with clenched lips and swollen red eyes. Dusty was with him. The big guy's usual cheeriness was nowhere to be found. His ears flopped to the side in mulish fashion.

Mark knelt next to Jangles and ran his hands over the burro's body. "The animal tracks on the ranch looked a lot like wolverine tracks, but we're too far south

"Shouldn't there be blood all over the place?" Kenzie sniffed and wiped back a tear.

Mark took me from Kenzie. "I'm so glad you're alright. Looks like you were watching out for Jangles. You're a brave cat."

Well, that wasn't exactly true. I hadn't been looking out for Jangles—I'd been looking out for me.

Taking care of number one never bothered me before, but after everything that happened to the mice, and Jangles, I felt strangely selfish. My head found a nice spot to rub against Mark's shoulder. He felt warm and the ground had been hard and cold.

"It doesn't look like any kind of animal attack I've ever seen. We'll have the vet out...and probably the police."

CHAPTER 8

A Dark Moment

I wasn't sure what a vet was, but someone arrived in a big truck. When Mark spoke about the burro to the stranger, he whispered a lot.

"D-E-A-D," he said softly. "I don't want to upset the others any more than they are." His eyes were red and his tone quiet, especially whenever he mentioned Jangles by name.

Dusty, Daisy, and Red milled around the corral. The gate to go out from the corral into the pasture was open, but no one was going anywhere.

Dusty shifted about the corral. His ears flopped, and instead of the big grin he always had on his face, he frowned. The tips of his hooves clipped the ground every once in a while, as if he were sleepwalking.

Daisy's eyes watered. Every time Mark or Kenzie walked near her, she would call out. They would come over, and she would lean her head into their arms. Red stood around with his rubbery lips drooping in a loose pout. I think the horses were as broken up about Jangles as Mark was. Did everyone forget the burro was also working with Magus? Surely Dusty told Daisy and Red all of what happened. Then again, what did I know? I was just the victim here.

The door to the house was conveniently left open, and I made my way inside to throw myself into a long day's sleep. As I walked in, my heart skipped several beats. The moonstone lay in a heap on the floor beneath the table, broken into three pieces. This wasn't good. No wonder Dusty was upset. He must not have stopped Magus's black spot.

A slow once-over of the rock and not a single shape on its surface moved. There was no buzz, and my tail wouldn't tingle. Whatever made the stone feel alive was gone. A chill raced through me, and it wasn't caused by the dangly around my neck. There would be nothing to keep Magus and the weasels out now.

"What do you say, cat?" the fat mouse asked.

I nearly jumped out of my skin.

"Was our information good?"

"Do you ever knock?" I asked.

The fat mouse eyed me with his beady black eyes, but didn't answer.

"Yes," I said. "We have a deal, for all the good it's going to do you."

"Okay, gang, bring it in." The scrawny mouse showed up leading ten mice. "Heave, ho, heave, ho," he squeaked.

The mice dragged a circular piece of metal along the ground by a long ribbon. It had that Lisa smell on it. Since the mice looked as if getting the medal to me would take forever, I went over and grabbed it with my teeth. The dangly on my collar went wild, swinging to and fro. This might be interesting.

"Lisa said you had to give this to Dusty if something ever happened to the stone. It has to come from you. She gave us strict instructions to be sure you got it."

The metal circle lit up like a full moon on a clear night. I dropped it and brushed over the piece with my paw. A small Lisa-shaped image popped out from it. It gave off a soft light, just like the moon.

"Kitten, if the mice brought this to you, the worst has happened. The stone is broken and the moon is waning, so coming to you will be dangerous for everyone since I haven't the strength to take on Magus in a face-to-face fight. When Jangles betrayed you, the ranch family crumbled, and so did the stone. The stone wasn't powered only by moonlight, it was also powered by the sense of family. It will only be a matter of time before Magus attacks you all directly."

I moved closer and took a sniff at the little image and passed my paw through it. It wasn't solid.

"When I saw into the future of this ranch," the image continued. "All of the possibilities looked bleak. Introducing you to the mix brought in new possibilities. The death of one of you, and the stone breaking, was one possible outcome that might happen," the figure said. "All is not lost. The future may still be changed to a positive outcome. That is why I brought you here. Dusty will need you. The stone may be mended, or replaced, but it must be done before the new moon. If the new moon comes before the stone is repaired, Dusty and Daisy must be returned. That is provided Magus hasn't gotten them first. You don't have much time."

"Wait." My paw passed through the figure. I have some questions."

The figure spoke again, "Magus knows the stone can be mended or replaced, and he will lie in wait for Dusty and you. Give Dusty this medallion. It is up to Daisy and Dusty to leave or fight."

The image faded out of view.

I pounded my paw on the medallion. "Wait! What's a new moon? How do we fix the stone?"

The medallion lay on the floor, still and lifeless. I glared at the fat mouse. "Mouse, do you know?"

He shrugged.

I flicked my tail and showed him all of my teeth. The little rodent cringed.

"We have a deal, cat, remember?" he squeaked.

"Keep your tail on, I know. I have to speak to Grass Bag.

If I need you, how do I contact you?"

He twitched his nose and whiskers. "No need, we always know."

There was a knock at the door, and a stranger wearing brown shorts and shirt stepped inside. He carried a box that was a little bigger than me.

Mark stepped in behind him. "May I help you?" "A delivery."

Mark signed something for the man, and the man handed off the box and left the house.

"I didn't order anything." Mark set the box on the table.

My tail went crazy. The hair puffed out, and the dangly thing around my neck went frigid.

He cut open the box and pulled out a funny-looking halter like the horses wear, but made for a smaller, bullet-shaped head.

I broke one of Dusty's rules.

"Mark! Noooooo!"

Too late.

CHAPTER 9

An Even Darker Moment

Mark wasn't Mark anymore. He stood near the dining room on four stick-thin legs. Attached to those legs were round, soft feet. Each foot had two large toes. His horseshoe- shaped neck was long and unattractive. With his new padded knees, shoulders, and chest, he looked like a strange version of Jangles without the long ears. In fact, his ears were small and didn't fit his new, long and narrow head.

Mark's new lips were as rubbery as Red's, but only half the size. There was a big hump in the middle of his back, which made his ears look even smaller. There was no telling what Mark had become. He was scary, but not as scary as his smell. His new stink was a force to be reckoned with. To think I complained about Grass Bag and company. This could only be the work of Magus.

"I need to get out of here," I said. "This is too weird."

"Raaaaaa. Raaaaaaa," Mark groaned. His clothes started to shrink, and for a moment, I thought they would tear off. His pants and shirt soaked up into his new fur the way a cloth might soak up water.

Kenzie stepped through the door, "Mark, the vet is gone and..."

"Oh, mouse droppings." I said. And no, I didn't say meow, or half a dozen other sounds humans associate with cute cats. I spoke human. "Mouse droppings!"

Kenzie's eyes went wide and then narrowed into a squint, but then she caught sight of Mark's new form and let out an ear- splitting scream before she crumpled onto the dining room floor.

Could things get any worse?

The mice scampered to the barn to retrieve the horses, and I stayed with Mark. Not that there was much I could do.

Everyone arrived at once. Red opened the front door so Dusty and company could come in. Wow! Those big, rubber lips of his were useful after all.

"What in the name of alfalfa?" Dusty's eyes blazed and his ears flicked forward as he went into protection mode.

Daisy let out a window-rattling call, and Red trotted over to give the camel a welcoming taste. His big lips wrapped around the camel's tail, but the camel jerked free and bit him. That should teach old rubber-lips.

"Kitten?" Dusty bellowed. "Where's Mark?"

"You're looking at him." I nodded in the direction of old knobby-knees.

Daisy brushed Kenzie's cheek and forehead with her muzzle, whickered to her brother, and peered back at Kenzie.

The girl stirred.

"Mark?" Kenzie stared at us. "What are all of you doing inside the house? You're not supposed to be in here." She rubbed her head. "I could have sworn there was a camel in the living room and that Kitten spoke to me."

I flicked a message with my tail to the big guy. "Are you going to tell her?"

Dusty snorted and shook his head, but Daisy sighed and nodded.

"Okay," Dusty said. "Kenzie, we have a secret, but you can't tell anyone."

Kenzie's face went as pale as the moon in late afternoon. Her eyes threatened to roll back in her head as if she were going to pass out again.

Dusty stomped his foot against the floor.

"None of that," he said. "We need you to stay alert."

Kenzie focused on Daisy's face. "Do you speak too?"

Daisy whickered and shook her head.

Mark groaned a camel sound and started tasting the couch cushions. Kenzie's eyes widened. "Oh, no."

"Maybe we should move this conversation to the barn," Dusty said. "We don't want any accidents on the carpet." The big guy moved to the door and called out, "Follow us."

The camel fell into step behind Dusty, and the rest of us followed the camel.

"What is going on? Since when have you all been able to talk? Can you understand everything I say?" Kenzie's face went red. "I...I...I can't believe I told you about how much I liked Gary...I'm so never talking to you again, Dusty."

Kenzie plunked down on a bale of hay as the big guy winked at me. He gave me the grin and flicked his ears. That meant it was up to me to calm her down.

"Kenzie." I jumped up on the bale next to her. "Please don't be angry, and don't be scared. It's still us. To be truthful, I really didn't know I could talk to anyone, or anything, until I got here. I've lived by myself for a long time and never noticed. I suppose we were going to have to tell Mark eventually, especially since the moonstone is broken. Things are about to get worse."

"What's that got to—Oh." Kenzie's gaze shifted from Dusty then to me. "Is that camel supposed to be Mark?" Kenzie's eyes went wide.

"It's worse than that," Dusty said.

"Mark is a camel. How much worse can it be? Oh wait, the bill of sale." She looked at Dusty. "If the stone is broken, Mark can't keep you anymore." She pressed her hand to her forehead. "No...this is all stupid. Horses and cats don't talk. Mark's pranking me, and he's recording all this to post online."

"Horses and cats can too talk," Dusty said. "Just not to other species. Me and Kitten are the exception. We not only talk, but we can understand when other animals talk back."

Daisy nuzzled Kenzie. "Daisy doesn't seem to talk.

128

Does she understand?"

Dusty leaned into his sister. "Mostly. She has other gifts." Kenzie's face kept changing from pale to red to pink and pale again, all within seconds. Her hands shook and so I got onto her lap and purred to calm her down.

Kenzie stroked my head. "Changing a person into an animal is straight out of fairy tales. It doesn't really happen, does it?"

"What's a fairy tale?" I asked. "Is that like a cat's tail or a horse's tail? That reminds me. Dusty, Lisa left something for you. While I go get it, can you catch Kenzie up?"

When I got back, Mark was chowing down on hay. Kenzie's eyes were still wide, and her lips were clenched in a straight line.

I set the medallion on the bale, touched Kenzie's leg with my paw. and winked at her. In one quick leap, I was next to her, bumping her hand with my head.

"What's that?" Dusty asked.

"Before I tell you," I answered. "I want to know what happened when you took off after the big glob of ooze."

"I failed." The big guy dropped his head low and flattened his ears sideways.

So, I guess horses can look sheepish after all.

"The glob?" Kenzie asked.

"Yeah. Did Dusty explain how Jangles was killed?" She sniffed and brushed a tear back. "Yes."

Dusty's voice wobbled. "I lost the thing in the brush. When I went back to the pasture fence, it was slithering across the ground in the direction of the house. This all happened because Jangles betrayed us." He blew out a gusty sigh. "I jumped the fence to get it, but it was too fast. The door to the house was open before I even got halfway. By the time I arrived there, the ooze had slipped back out and vanished. I didn't go inside. I already knew what had happened. I felt the moonstone break."

"How?" Kenzie asked.

"Being here on the ranch always felt warm and comfortable, but a cold feeling deep inside replaced that." Dusty hung his head. "Daisy and I must go away—that was the deal."

"That's silly." Kenzie stroked my head. "How can anyone know the stone is broken besides us?"

I batted at the medallion on Kenzie's knee. "How can a cat and a horse talk to a human?" I asked.

"What is that thing?" Dusty asked.

"I don't know. Lisa popped out of it and said to give it to you." A yawn worked its way out. I really needed a nap.

"But Lisa only comes out with the moon."

"She sends Grimalkin to do her errands during the day," I explained. "I'm pretty sure he'll be here soon."

Kenzie tilted her head to look me in the face. "Who?"

"Yeah, who is Grimalkin?" Dusty blinked at me.

"He's the one who gave me the sparkly thing." I raised my chin and shown off my collar. "Just after we dealt with the flying weasels. He's the one who told me how to take care of those nasty things."

"Weasels aren't nasty," Kenzie said. "Weasels are just animals."

Dusty shifted his weight. "Kitten actually meant wentzels. He just calls them that..."

I gave the big guy a look.

"We call them weasels at Kitten's urging," Dusty said.

"And it's a good thing you do," a voice spoke from the doorway. "If you didn't, they'd be ten times worse."

CHAPTER 10

The Meeting

Grimalkin sauntered in as if he owned the world, just as any cat would. After all, we do own the world—we just let everyone else live here.

The gray cat peered at us unblinking.

"Well now, if this isn't nice and cozy. Are we having tea?" he asked.

"Who are you?" Dusty glared at the new cat. The big guy laid his ears flat and his gaze flashed fire.

"That's Grimalkin," I said. "He's kin of mine, sort of. He helped me with the flying weasels the other day."

"Well, I wouldn't say I exactly helped." Grimalkin stopped to yawn. "You did the hard work."

"Flying weasels?" Kenzie stood up. "What?"

"Sit down, girl," Grimalkin snapped. "Be still and all will be explained."

"That would be a nice change," I added. "Someone actually explaining things instead of talking about vague rules," I yawned back. What can I say? Yawning is a cat thing.

Dusty snorted. "Get on with it."

"When the earth was very young there used to be many of us." Grimalkin made his way to the hay bale. "If I were to explain it in a way that is easy for you to understand, think of us as guardians or helpers. For as long as we've been around, we have tried to nudge things in better directions. We like to help where we can." Grimalkin licked his lips.

"So?" Kenzie shrugged. "How about a little help?"

"Things don't work quite that way," he said. "We are long-lived, but not immortal. Eventually, we fade and become something different. Many of my kind—Lisa-types, as Kitten likes to say—have moved on." Grimalkin hopped up on the bale next to Kenzie. "May I sit here?"

Grimalkin took up too much space, so I hopped down.

"What does this have to do with the moonstone, Dusty, Daisy, and everything else?" Kenzie asked.

"I bet, girl, you are the kind that reads the end of a book first." He sat and blinked. "May I be allowed to continue without interruption?"

"Please," Dusty said.

"My kind have managed a great many things and helped here and there when the rules allowed. I admit, the rules can be rather tiresome at times, even for the best of us."

"Magus?" I asked.

"This wasn't his original name, but it would be wise to limit how much we mention any of his names." Grimalkin lay down next to Kenzie. "Names are very powerful things. You all would do well to remember that."

"Maggot?" Dusty asked.

"You're a horse after my own heart." Grimalkin twitched his whiskers and sneezed. "Kenzie, darlin', would you be so kind as to scratch behind my ears, please."

"Fine, if it will hurry you up, so you can get on with it."

"The Maggot, to borrow the big fella's phrase, is trying to prove a point. The Grand Shadowness wants to cheat his fate and will unleash a misery upon this world as a result."

"Dusty and I heard Maggot tell Jangles he wasn't interested in me and Dusty anymore, other than to cause problems."

Grimalkin blinked. "The Maggot extends his existence by consuming his own kind. He'd eat me if he could, but I'm a lot more fight and bother than he wants to deal with for now. Lisa would be easier prey as she is showing her age these days, especially when the moon is waning."

"Couldn't he just eat you and then go away?" Kenzie asked.

"No. The only other suitable food for him is human emotion, preferably misery and suffering. There was a big fight among my kind long ago, and he sort of lost."

"I bet Maggot figured out that once he ate all of you, there would be nothing left to feed on," Dusty added.

"Right you are, Boyo. At least he did eventually. That was when he developed a taste for human misery. It's not as potent, so he has to eat a lot, but it is substituted in our place." Grimalkin paused, yawned, and continued. "Kenzie, a little more to the left please. Thank you. Those of us who are still around try to keep the Maggot on a tight leash, but we have to be careful not to get eaten ourselves. As a result, we've resorted to using individuals you might think of as heroes."

"Like Dusty?" I asked. "Lisa called him heroic."

Grimalkin nodded. "The right individual has the ability to borrow just enough from us, harness that, and become something a little more than who they were."

"How come Daisy and I had never seen Maggot until Kitten arrived?" Dusty shifted his position and moved a little closer.

"Maggot...oh, I do really like that! I'm surprised I didn't think of it." He started to purr. "Lisa's stone hid you, among other things. Not so long ago, Maggot figured out that if he consumes a hero, he gets a direct link to our energy. He doesn't have to eat us or fight us that way. He uses the link and feeds at will. We had to abandon the use of champions a long time ago, except on rare occasions." He yawned. "Thank you, Kenzie.

Kenzie gave him a disbelieving look. "Are you going to take a nap or help?"

Grimalkin straightened and shook his head. "Sorry, it's usually my nap time about now."

Dusty snorted.

"Moving on. So, we started using tokens. Like Lisa's moonstone, and the sparkly around Kitten's neck. They store a bit of us in them. You don't need to share a direct link with us anymore if you have our tokens."

Kenzie wrinkled her brow. "Let me get this straight. Maggot used heroes like a straw to feed on you? So, you made powerful gadgets for your heroes to draw on instead of linking them to you. If Maggot gets a hero, he only gains the energy from the token."

"Exactly. Your ear scratching was acceptable."

"Magus wanted to eat Kitten." Dusty pawed the ground. "Has that changed?"

"Yes and no, Dusty," Grimalkin said. "Old Maggot has a nasty streak. Lisa and I believe he has another plan now. There is no point to eating a hero anymore, other than for spite and to snack on their token. Believe it or not, us guardians agonize over the loss of our heroes. Losing one of them causes us centuries of sadness."

I flicked my tail. "I bet Maggot feeds on your misery too."

"Oh, yes. He finds it far more nourishing than human misery. This made our champions even more of a target. After all, we do get attached to them."

Kenzie shifted herself on the bale. "All the time I've worked for Mark, none of this has ever shown up. Why now?"

"Like I said, Lisa's fabulous stone has kept the brother and sister hidden. That protection ended the moment the moonstone broke, so I am here to collect Dusty and Daisy."

"What?" Dusty said.

Kenzie snapped her fingers. "That's what the bill of sale meant. If the stone is broken, Dusty and Daisy can't live here anymore...because they're not safe."

"Why didn't the moonstone stop that thing Maggot set loose last night?" Dusty asked.

"Jangles made a deal with Maggot—oh, that name just rolls off the tongue. The villain, in turn, chewed off the burro's essence and infused it into himself. Your community was broken the minute Jangles's essence went into the old villain." Grimalkin stood up. "Enough chit-chat. Let's go."

Daisy snorted, shook her head, and pawed the ground.

"What did she say?" Kenzie asked.

"She doesn't want to go," I said. "And she couldn't believe Jangles betrayed everyone."

Grimalkin sighed. "Oh, dearie, somewhere in Jangles, the Maggot found a pool of sorrow to twist."

"He was Maggot's chosen." Dusty bowed his head.

"Yes," Grimalkin agreed.

"But the token?" I added. "It wasn't supposed to allow..."

"Jangles came to the ranch as a rescue animal," Kenzie said. "Mark opened his home to him. His old owner was so cruel."

"He was doing so good, too." Dusty's eyes started to tear. "I thought he was..."

"I know lad, you and this family have a lot of compassion. It's why the moonstone has been so effective for so long. Maggot still had a few hooks into Jangles. Maggot is very good at corrupting things."

"He sounds like a parasite," Kenzie said.

"Exactly." Grimalkin jumped off the bale. "Since the stone is broken, I've come to collect Dusty and Daisy. A deal is a deal."

Kenzie jumped up from the bale and blocked his path. "What about Mark? You can't leave him like that! Can't you turn him back?"

"No." Grimalkin moved around her.

"I want to talk to this Lisa," Kenzie said.

"Sorry, it's too risky. An ambush has been set—can't you feel it?"

"We have until the new moon," I said. "That's what the medallion told me. They have until the new moon before

141

they have to be returned."

Kenzie held up the medallion. "Isn't there a way?"

"You would have to bring that up." Grimalkin shook his head and sauntered toward the door. "Fine, you win. Do both of you really want to be eaten?"

"What if we fixed the stone?" Dusty asked. "Mark fixes stuff all the time."

"Yes, if you must know," Grimalkin said. "Kitten, when did Lisa send you here? What was the moon like?"

"It wasn't full. It had been full, but it was still pretty full," I said.

"Many refer to that stage as waning gibbous." Grimalkin reached the threshold. "Time has passed, and as of today, we are just beyond the waning crescent stage. The next stage is the new moon. I don't have to collect Dusty and Daisy today, but if you two horses are daft enough to stick it out until the new moon, there is a way."

"What do you mean by that?" Dusty asked.

As quickly as Grimalkin had appeared, he disappeared. Poof.

"Where'd he go?" Kenzie asked. "What are we supposed to do now?"

I stood next to Dusty. "Why didn't you go? You could have been safe."

"Remember what I said to you the evening you came to us?" Dusty's nose hovered above my head, and his warm breath flowed around me.

"Yes, every word, especially about being afraid," I answered.

"How do you feel right now, Kitten?"

My stomach felt as if I had swallowed ten mice, and they weren't planning on staying in there.

"Afraid. Really afraid."

"Then being here has done wonders for you. You've learned to care. I'm staying because I'm afraid. This is my home and it's worth fighting for."

Daisy came up on my other side and gave me a friendly nudge.

I rubbed my head against her nose. "Um, what's a new moon?"

Kenzie pulled her phone from her pocket and started tapping on it. She studied the shiny side for a moment.

"When there is no moon to be seen from the Earth's surface that is the new moon. We've already started the final week leading up to it. We have three days as of tomorrow. I just looked it up on my phone."

At that moment, my tail fluffed out. "Something bad is outside."

"We call them weasels," said Dusty. His grin as large as ever. "We don't call them wentzels anymore, they're weasels. I have it on good authority that mispronouncing names is able to drain power from the fiercest of creatures. It's also fun to mess with their names too."

Daisy moved to the barn door and let out a call that rattled the rafters.

Kenzie stood and turned the barn light on. The sun was falling fast from the sky, and the small sliver of moon had set in the early afternoon, not due to rise again until the wee small hours. We poked our heads outside the barn door.

A huge animal ambled through the pasture toward us.

Dusty's whisper gave me the creeps. "That weasel's as big as a grizzly bear."

It was true. The monster had the usual weasel body, spine showing in the middle. But its paws were large enough to wrap around Dusty and Daisy in one grip.

Kenzie wrapped her arms around her middle as if she were sick to her stomach. "If that's a weasel, it's different than I pictured."

This weasel was unlike any before, and I thought the flying ones were weird. The head on this one was identical to Jangles's head. I assumed it was Maggot's way of rubbing salt in the wounds of Dusty's loss. The other thing, this one was ginormous. I looked up at Dusty. "Sorry you didn't leave when you had the chance?"

CHAPTER 11

Attack of the Beasel

You should have gone with Grimalkin," I said.

Daisy gave me a shove with her nose.

"Hey." I batted back but didn't use my claws.

"Daisy and I are not leaving you or Mark." Dusty stomped his feet and snorted. "Mark is a part of us, just like you, Kitten. This is our home and family."

The sparkly on my collar went crazy with movement. It also felt cold. "I hate this thing around my neck. Grimalkin never told me what this actually does. It doesn't seem to work like the moonstone."

"Rawwwrrrrr," Mark said as he joined us.

"That's a good idea, Mark." Dusty flicked his ears and swished his tail.

"You understood that?" I asked.

Daisy let loose with one loud whinny, which I took for a yes.

"Mark thinks that thing around your neck might help you fight the weasel." Dusty faced out the door.

"Mark called it a weasel, right? Not a Jangzel?" I flashed the camel a suspicious look.

Daisy snorted.

"You aren't going to fight that thing, are you?" Kenzie

strode to the door and went to slide it shut. "It's vicious! Besides, Jangles was one of us. Using even a part of his name for that thing is wrong."

"I agree," I said. "We won't use Jangles's name."

Daisy touched Kenzie's cheek and let out a soft breath. The girl didn't close the door, instead drops of water trickled from her eyes.

"That settles it, we call it a beasel," I said. "It's got a burro head, and big weasel body."

"How can you talk like this?" Kenzie sniffed. "This may not be Jangles, but the head looks like him."

"No, that's not our Jangles. Beasel it is." Dusty pushed through the door and lit out towards the thing, shouting, "Beasel Burgers!"

Daisy raced out on his heels with Mark behind her.

"I think I'm rubbing off on the big guy, and in a good way." I went to run too, but Kenzie grabbed me by the scruff of my neck.

"Hey," I said.

"No you don't, you're too small." Kenzie reached for my collar. "Besides, I have an idea, but I need to get that collar off."

"Augh." A gasp choked out of me as she struggled to get it off.

"Big baby, hold still," she said.

It's amazing how easy the collar slipped off over my head, like it was made to do that, whew!

"I'm pretty sure this thing works like a prism," Kenzie offered. "There's something I learned from my mom about diffusing light and shadows." Kenzie fingered my collar in her hand. "If I were to believe that goofy talking cat, I think Mag...Maggot, the huge shadow, has his hands full dealing with Lisa because she uses soft light."

"Light is always soft," I said, now that I was free.

"No, not soft or hard like when you get punched. My mom is a video editor and deals with lighting all day long. The moon doesn't create light like the sun. It reflects light from the sun, so the light from the moon isn't as bright because it's diffusing the sunlight. If you don't want a light to cast a shadow in a studio, you diffuse it by shining it through something to soften it. Hard light, like the sun makes, creates shadows. If Maggot is a shadow and uses shadows, the sunlight isn't going to bother him, it will help him. If you want to get rid of a shadow, use soft light."

"I have no idea what you're talking about," I said.

Kenzie walked to the little cupboard on the wall and flipped the lights off. She grabbed the flashlight from the cupboard, grasped the collar in one hand and shone light through the sparkly on the collar.

My token was the size of a pea and had lots of angled edges on it. When the light went through it, a cloud of sparkles exploded inside the barn.

"No shadows, right?" Kenzie said.

Dusty let out a yell and we heard a loud thump against the side of the barn, followed by a cry from Daisy. Mark was growling and spitting, almost like a cat.

"That doesn't sound good," I said.

Kenzie rushed to the barn door and peered out. Dusty had been knocked down and lay against the barn, a gash in his shoulder and side. Daisy gave the beasel both barrels and connected her back feet square into its side. The beasel bounced sideways and fell to the ground. It grabbed a wooden rail of the fence, stood, and staggered several steps. It wasn't fazed for long. It took one quick glance at Dusty lying on the ground and let out a raspy bray. My blood ran cold. The beasel was going in for the kill.

Kenzie held out my collar and shot the flashlight through the sparkly, but when the light went through this time, the cloud of sparkles didn't fill the corral. Hardly anything came out.

"We'll need to put Grimalkin's bauble closer," Kenzie said. "Closer to the—oh, all right, closer to the beasel."

"Are you crazy?" I asked. "Who's going to take it closer?"

Daisy let out a squeal.

The beasel rushed at Dusty. Something terrible was about to happen. I wanted to run and hide, to be anywhere but here. The beasel hadn't frightened me until it closed in on the big guy. The idea of something happening to Dusty froze me in my tracks.

"Kitten!" Kenzie shouted. "Take the bauble closer, put it right on him if you can. Do it now before it's too late." She dropped her hand low so I could take the collar in my teeth.

I was off in a flash. All the hesitation was gone. The burning desire to shout "Beasel burgers!" was overpowering, but I couldn't risk dropping the collar. In one flying leap, I scrambled up the beasel's back and side, rushing toward its face.

"Dangle it in front of the eyes," Kenzie shouted.

Miss Smartphone sure was expecting a lot, wasn't she? The miserable thing jostled and honked, making it hard to hold on, even with my claws. Daisy let out a call, pleading to save her brother.

I clawed my way toward the burro's head and threaded myself between the creature's long ears.

"Drape it across one of the eyes, Kitten," Kenzie shouted. Easy for her to say, she has thumbs. Somehow, I draped myself across the wide forehead and dangled the sparkly before the eye closest to Kenzie while holding the collar in my teeth.

"Rrrrrowrrrr," I yowled.

Kenzie hit the beasel in the eye with a beam of light just as I draped the token in front of it. Hopefully, it was too stupid to close its eye.

The white beam of the flashlight hit the bauble and split into a rainbow of colors, filling the gruesome thing's eye. The beasel groaned but didn't move. The explosion of sparkling colors froze it in mid-stride. In a twitch of a whisker, its body quivered and softened beneath my claws. Before I could jump off, its mass melted into an enormous pile of gristle and shrank into the ground with me landing in it. The collar fell to pieces in my mouth and I gagged on a few scraps that found their way down my throat.

"I'm not going to lick myself clean after this," I said. "That is just too gross."

"Way to go, Kitten!" Kenzie didn't seem to care about the slime.

Dusty let out a squeal but wasn't getting up. Daisy rushed over to him and kept him from trying. A long, bloody gash ran the full length of the big guy's side from shoulder to rump. Red blood oozed from the wound and stained his yellow coat. Daisy nuzzled her brother's cheek.

She snorted and pressed her nose towards Dusty's shoulder where the gash began.

Dusty winced.

The moon was nowhere to be seen. Daisy cast a quick glance at the sky and sighed. She breathed in and out, her sides heaving, but as she did, the outline of a crescent slice glowed into life on her forehead. The gash on Dusty's side knit itself together and faded.

"Whoa," Kenzie said. "Where's my phone, I need to video this. Wait, I should have taken a picture of the whole thing." She slapped her forehead. "What was I thinking?"

"You were thinking about staying alive, maybe?" I asked.

Dusty let out a moan, and as he did the gash faded completely from sight leaving only bloodstains in its place. He gathered his legs under him and was back on his feet in a moment.

"Thank you, Kitten and Kenzie," Dusty said. "That's the first time Daisy has ever been able to do that without the moon present. Kitten, where's your token?"

I shrugged.

"I'm sorry," he added. "Such tokens don't come easy and I bet they are seldom replaced."

"It was worth it. The beasel was annoying."

"Guys," Kenzie screeched. "Quick, look."

She pulled the medallion from her pocket and placed it in the flat of her hand. A full-size Lisa appeared hovering above us. She was thin and wrinkly like some old human.

Her hair was silver-white, but her eyes still shone with the same yellow- orange glow I remembered from when we first met.

"Well done, my heroes. I could not have hoped for a better outcome." Her face turned to Dusty and Daisy. "I knew you would not want to leave Mark once you went to live with him, but if you're seeing this, my stone is broken. You have one chance to repair it. Take it to the forest people in a place the humans call the Kiamichi Mountains. Get them to mend the stone, or maybe they can give you a new one."

"That's where Mark was going," Kenzie said. "He said something about Bigfoot."

Lisa turned to Kenzie and smiled. "Same thing."

"There is a way?" Dusty grinned.

"Yes," Lisa said. "Beware, the Magus will be waiting for you. He knows all about the stone and who can repair it." The figure flickered. "You all must stand together as one community back here on the property by sunrise on the day of the new moon. If you do not, Grimalkin will have to remove Dusty and Daisy."

The horses tensed up at that statement. Wanting to

stay in your home was something I knew all about. After all, Lisa did force me to move from my home to wherever this was.

"Collect everything you will need for your journey," Lisa added. "Raise the medallion toward the rising crescent and you will be transported to where you must go. Good fortune to you all and beware the Magus. He will be waiting."

The image disappeared.

"We have an adventure to prepare for." Dusty cleared his throat. "Kenzie, I saw you driving the other truck, do you think you can drive Mark's good one?"

"Oh yeah!" Kenzie replied, a grin stretching from ear to ear. "I was born to drive that truck."

"Rwwwaawwwwawww," Mark complained.

"Zip it, Mr. Peterson." Kenzie shushed Mark. "Do you really want to stay a camel for the rest of your life?"

Kenzie fed us all. Miss Smartphone also used Mark's cell to text her parents and let them know that Mark got some last-minute instructions from the company that hired him. He would have to leave sometime after midnight because of contract requirements for his job.

Dusty asked Kenzie to keep the medallion in her pocket since she was the only one of us wearing pants.

"We need to be ready in a few hours. The crescent moon appears just before dawn. We have to pack the trailer now," Dusty said. "We've got to be ready by the rising moon."

Kenzie's thumb flew in a flurry of movements across the face of her phone. "I let my parents know that Mark's timetable just got moved up on his job and we have to leave in a few hours. They seem to be okay with that. Mom's going to pack my clothes for me. Let me go pick them up and I'll come back to get us packed." Kenzie said, turning to cross the pasture toward her home.

Dusty grabbed my tail as I watched her leave. I didn't jump out of my skin this time.

"Will you stop that?" I gazed back at the Grass Bag.

"No," Dusty replied. "You know I can't let you come with us. Julie will take care of you and Red. I told Kenzie to text her..."

"Oh no," I said.

"No arguments. Your token is gone."

"So is yours," I argued.

"We're going to try and get ours repaired. I couldn't live with myself if something happened to you because of me." His eyes teared a little. "I let Jangles down, but I won't do that with you. Mark, Daisy, and me, we've had our share of adventures. If we fail, Mark and us can live in the Kiamichis. Those mountains are no place for a cat."

"Well, Mr. I-can't-take-care-of-you, did you ever think this wasn't all about you? Maybe you need someone to watch your back more than I need to be taken care of. Besides, this place and you all are my home now."

Dusty blinked and didn't say another word. He could think whatever he wanted. There was no way I was staying behind.

CHAPTER 12

The Moon Tunnel

Kenzie shoved boxes of stuff into the storage area of the trailer. She returned and packed everything we needed with very little help from us. After all, cats and horses have good sense and no thumbs. A human's best qualities are their thumbs so they can work can openers and feed bags.

Mark bossed everyone around with his camel noises. Dusty quit translating after the first ten minutes. As far as the important stuff like hay bags, grain, brushes, and other items for the horses, Kenzie said Mark always kept it packed and ready to go in the horse trailer. His job often required him to pack up and go at moment's notice.

The dark night sky twinkled with stars and the tiny sliver of moon finally made an appearance.

Mark was still spitting and honking all over the place so Kenzie put him in the barn.

"You'd think he'd be more docile as a camel," I said to Kenzie. "Shouldn't Mark be left here too?"

"No," Dusty shouted. "We're partners. It's not an adventure without Mark."

"Well if you haven't noticed, this is more life and death than an adventure." Kenzie flashed her cell phone. "I

Googled camels last night. They aren't known for their sweet disposition."

"I think Mark is very sweet as humans go," I said, making sure to stand on the saddle blanket Kenzie was about to pick up. Kenzie yanked it out from beneath me and toted it to the storage space inside the front of the trailer. "There's plenty of room for Dusty and Daisy, but the trailer was made for four horses, not two horses and a camel."

"Daisy and I will take the one side," Dusty said. "Mark will have to squeeze into the other. You have the backup person coming for Red and Kitten?"

"For the tenth time, yes. Julie will be here later. I've used Mark's phone to send texts back and forth to my folks and to Julie. None of them know Mark can't drive. It did take some fast explaining as to why we aren't leaving at a more reasonable time."

Dusty snorted. "It's not right to lie to your parents, Kenzie.

You need to tell them the truth."

"Right," she said. "Mark got turned into a camel because there's a monster that wants to eat you, Daisy, and Mark's new cat. Once he eats them he can feed off the nearly-immortal life force of a fairy and a magical cat." Kenzie rolled her eyes. "Yeah, like that's really going to fly. Besides, it's not like I'm breaking the law, exactly. Mark is a licensed driver and my permit allows me to drive as long as I have Mark with me." She gazed down at me. "That's why Mark must come, so I don't break the law."

Dusty snorted. He didn't believe her, but he wasn't going to argue either.

"I still don't know why Daisy gets to go and I don't," I said.

"She always goes with us. Everywhere Mark and I go. She works hard and packs things about. As for you, the mountains aren't safe for a house cat. There's too many things there that can eat you."

"Well, that's true about this place too, now that there's no moonstone," I argued. "Don't forget I lost my token because of you. What's to say weasels won't come looking for me once you're gone?"

"Well, that would be a good thing, wouldn't it?" Dusty grinned. "More weasels we won't have to deal with. Hey, at least I stopped calling them wentzels."

Kenzie pulled the medallion from her pocket. "How is this supposed to work? What makes you think it's going to move all of us together?"

"I don't know, let's get ready and see what happens," Dusty said.

"Yes, it was a good thing I found the key to the camper shell in the glove box in the truck," Kenzie added. "How does Mark find anything in his house?"

Kenzie opened the trailer and the side feed doors. Dusty shifted to the entrance and stepped up and into the trailer, allowing Kenzie to hook his halter to the metal ring with a trailer tie. Daisy followed suit to the space behind him.

Mark was another story. Once Dusty and Daisy were in,

Mark dashed for the open driver's door of the pickup. When he put a front foot in the truck, it sank beneath his weight. Then he pushed his camel his camel head and neck inside.

"Mark!" Kenzie hollered. "You can't drive. You don't have hands and you won't fit!"

Mark let out a groan that shook the branches of a

nearby tree. His mouth quirked and twisted a huge foamy glob of spit.

"Don't you spit at me Mr. Peterson. You just keep it up and I will turn around and go home. Then how will you get to Oklahoma?"

"Rwawrrrrrrt," Mark groaned.

"Zip it! I won't hurt your truck. It won't get a scratch, I promise."

Dusty let out a bellow from inside the trailer.

Then Mark cut loose his wad of spit that hit the side of the barn.

Thunk!

I was sure that could be heard for miles.

Mark turned and slunk toward the trailer, his camel grumble sounding like a load of gravel scraping the bed of a truck.

"Keep it up Mr. Peterson. One more word and I'm going to wash your mouth out with non-foaming detergent."

Once everyone was in the trailer, Kenzie stopped and looked one last time at the open tailgate at the rear of the truck. She shifted her back to me and the truck and gazed at the barn, then the house, and Red in the corral. I scooted through the window between the truck and camper shell and nestled beneath under a blanket on the passenger's side. There was a fold perfect for peeking through.

Kenzie climbed in. "If for some reason Kitten has stowed away, and I'm not saying he did, he should stay quiet and hidden until I'm sure there's no way to send him back. Clear?"

The door closed, she stuck the key in the ignition and turned it—nothing happened.

"Well," she said. "What do we do now?"

She reached for her pocket and the medallion tucked inside.

"I wonder if I should put this in drive before..." The engine started on its own.

I didn't see what happened next other than Kenzie shifting to pull the medallion from her pocket.

The truck bounced up and down. Kenzie screamed, and the truck lurched forward and jerked to a stop.

"That's right," Kenzie said. "Put your foot on the brake and then shift into drive."

From under the blanket, it was easy to see her foot move off the brake. The truck lurched forward with a jerk and lifted upward.

My stomach jumped and rolled around my innards.

The blanket flew off. "Kitten, you've got to see this, quick."

The truck and trailer shot forward and upward on a glossy yellow-white road into a golden tunnel.

The sides of the tunnel were full of sparkly bits and shiny rocks. Streaks of silver and gray traced the road before us as we moved faster and faster.

My foot found the electric window switch. I rolled it down and stuck my head out. I mean, why should dogs have all the fun?

"Weasel Burgers!" I yelled.

Kenzie grinned at me. "Beasel Burgers!"

CHAPTER 13

Into The Kiamichi Mountains

The truck shot from Lisa's moon tunnel and raced toward a stand of pine saplings. A big explosion erupted beneath the front end.

BANG...whoosh...flap...flap...flap...flap.

Kenzie revved the truck with one step and held tight to the steering wheel as it nearly jerked loose from her grip.

"Hang on, Kitten!" Kenzie cried. "We just had a tire go flat."

Kenzie let off the go-faster pedal and held her foot down onto the thing she called a brake.

"We're going to run into the trees," I shouted.

"No, we won't," she replied through gritted teeth. "Top student in my Driver's Ed class, not to mention there are trailer brakes to help out."

She was right. The truck eased to a stop as a thud echoed from the trailer behind us, followed by a shrill call from Daisy. "Yeah, yeah. Everyone's a backseat driver," Kenzie griped.

Dust filled the cab through my open window.

"Oh yeah!" Kenzie screeched.

I sneezed.

For a moment, I expected the truck to swerve or slide, but what do I know about such things? Cats don't have to bother with such boring details. The truck did collapse a series of small saplings as we halted, but other than the explosion, we were in one piece. That's when I caught the soft glint of moonlight against the hood of the truck. Lisa had helped.

Kenzie's face beamed with accomplishment. She reminded me of a prize mouser in a barn that she'd cleared of rats. I don't think I'll mention the extra help.

"Wooot woooot!" Kenzie shouted. "Do it again."

Bang! Bang! Bang!

The noise came from Dusty's side of the trailer. The big guy sounded impatient.

He was right. We had a lot to do and very few nights of moonlight left. When the new moon arrived, leaving the night sky black, Grimalkin's pick-up service would collect Dusty and Daisy. That is, if they were still alive. Mark would be left as a camel and I was fair game for the Magus, or Maggot as Dusty called him. Even if the jerk told Jangles he wasn't interested in me anymore.

Kenzie reached down and threw a switch by the

steering wheel, flooding the night around us with light. "Mark put these in so we can see if anything is sneaking up on us in the dark." She opened the door. "You stay in the truck and out of sight while I let everyone out. Don't you dare show your whiskers until we're certain there's no way to send you back."

I flicked my tail and Kenzie nodded back. She would make an excellent cat.

The girl turned off the truck engine and vanished out the door. Soon I could hear the sliding of door latches and the banging of horse hooves against the trailer floor.

"Kenzie, what happened? Are we there?" Dusty demanded. I watched Kenzie through the side mirror as she opened the trailer feeding doors. She released Dusty and Daisy's trailer ties. Then she went to the other side and unlatched Mark's door.

A bullet of spit shot past her head.

"Oh, I didn't hurt your truck one bit, Mark Peterson."

"Raaaraaagh," Mark groaned.

"Mark, you are one grumpy camel." Kenzie undid his trailer tie and Mark backed out.

Mark joined the horses out by the cargo door at the

front of the trailer. Daisy stumbled a bit getting there, but then again, I might stumble too after Kenzie's drive through the tunnel of light.

Kenzie went to tie the horses to the trailer, but Dusty jerked his head high out of reach.

"You won't need that," he said. "We're not going anywhere until we're saddled."

"Yes sir!" Kenzie sassed back.

"Be sure you pack the pieces of stone in Daisy's saddle pack."

"Are you always this bossy? I think I liked you better when you didn't speak human."

"Include a day's worth of food and water for yourself. Daisy and I will be fine until we return to the truck."

"I know, Mr. Bossy. I've been on rides with you and Mark before," Kenzie huffed. "You know, you were a lot less demanding when I couldn't understand you."

Daisy said something that sounded like a cross between a whistle and a cough. It made me laugh.

Dusty snorted.

"What'd Daisy say?" Kenzie asked.

"I hope the Bigfoot aren't as shy as usual," Dusty

replied, changing the subject. "We need to find them quickly if we're to save Mark and our home. Maybe I was wrong to leave Kitten on the ranch. His tail may have saved us some time."

"You think so? You think Kitten is helpful?" Kenzie asked.

Dusty hesitated. "Yes, I do, but don't tell him I said that. We'll figure something out. Mark and I are used to being resourceful."

"I heard that, Grass Bag," I shouted as I jumped out of the truck.

"Dusty, about Kitten..." Kenzie started to speak.

The big guy cast his brown eyes on the camel and smiled, and somewhere down inside that mass of hair and foam-laden spit, Mark smiled back.

I rubbed my cheek against Daisy's front leg. Dusty tossed his head back and made a fair attempt at a scowl, but the big guy couldn't fool me. He was laughing too.

"Don't tell me you're angry to see me, Dusty," I said. "I heard what you said. Today, you're going to be glad that I have issues with authority."

Dusty rolled his eyes and snorted as Kenzie opened the

truck's tailgate.

"What's the plan?" I jumped up on the gate. "I presume Mark and Dusty are the experts on Bigfoot. Where do we find such animals in the mountains?"

"It's dark," Kenzie said. "We should wait until daylight."

Daisy stamped her feet and shook her head.

"Daisy is right." The big guy nodded. "The most promising eye-witness accounts happened during the night. Besides, we should have the crescent moon all morning in case we run across the Magus or weasels. Kenzie, do you have Lisa's medallion?"

Kenzie pulled the round piece of metal from her jeans pocket.

"Fasten that to my breast plate once you get me saddled. Mark keeps duct tape in the tool box. If the Bigfoot see it, they may not be so quick to hide. Bind it tight so it won't come off, but be sure we can take it off if we need to."

Dusty's eyes teared a little and he sighed. I wonder if he knew something he wasn't sharing.

"Yep, Mr. Bossy." Kenzie nodded and pulled out the

cell phones "No signal. Great."

"You should turn off the camp lights too," Dusty added. "We don't want the weasels to see us. If you need light, Mark keeps battery powered lanterns in the back of the truck."

I looked up at the thin sliver of light in the sky. It was only the barest of moons. According to Kenzie's earlier Google search, we had a few more nights of moonlight. How we were going to get back home, I didn't know. Worse yet, with the moon waning, Lisa's powers would be at their weakest and she wouldn't be much help. That round token looked so tiny as I thought more about possible weasels.

"What about the tire? Shouldn't I change it first?" Kenzie asked.

The big guy shook his head. "No time."

"But what if we have to move?" I asked. "How do you know this isn't..."

"I trust Lisa to get us where we needed to be."

"Raaaaaa," Mark said.

"Can you understand him, Dusty?" I asked. "He still makes no sense to me."

"Of course." Dusty's horsey grin expanded across his face. "Mark and I are partners. When we ride together, it's like he and I can read each other's minds. He's offering to carry the pack for Daisy."

CHAPTER 14

Weasels, Fuzzies, and Bear

Dusty charged through the brush and up an incline with Kenzie hanging tight in the saddle. I clung to the top of the canvas cover on Daisy's pack saddle as she followed behind. He didn't even ask me what direction I thought the Bigfoot might be. After a few paces, I heard nervous, twittering growls ahead.

Dusty shot towards the sound with Kenzie clinging to the saddle. Daisy and Mark loped after the big guy, hot on his heels. Me, I clung for my life to the canvas cover.

We came upon a small clearing and found three weasels in a semi-circle around a tall, furry human-thing. It looked a lot like Mark's fuzzy throw rug in his kitchen...if the rug was a very tall person.

It batted at the air in the direction of the weasels. The strikes weren't even close. They were unfocused and carried no real threat of claws or strength. I heard a low, thrumming noise vibrating from it and was sure everyone else could too, except maybe Kenzie.

Kenzie let out a screech. "We have to save it," she said. Her voice was high and shrill.

"Stay back, Daisy. Mark, with me!" Dusty let out a squeal and charged the weasels. Technically, so did

Kenzie, but then again, she was stuck to Dusty's back. "Hold tight, Kenzie. Weasel burgers!"

Daisy stumbled and stopped at the crest while Mark rushed on after the big guy, his camel mouth open as he groaned a war cry, probably his version of weasel burgers. Who would have guessed Mark had it in him?

Dusty pounced on weasel number one with all fours, squashing it like road kill. The medallion Kenzie had fastened to the breastplate flashed a bright silver streak of light and the creature dissolved into a smelly puddle of gristle. Kenzie clung to the saddle horn for all she was worth. Her face was drawn and her eyes wide.

"You got this, Kenzie," I yelled.

Weasel number two turned to slash Dusty's shoulder with a large right paw. I thought back to the corral and the wound the beasel inflicted on Dusty. He reared up on his back legs and caught the nasty thing in the face with an uppercut from his front hoof before the claws could touch him. The weasel fell backward, and Dusty drove both front hooves down into the weasel's chest. The medallion flashed silver and the weasel melted into the ground.

Weasel number three lunged at Dusty from behind, but Mark was ready.

I've never seen a camel in action, and I'm not sure Mark qualified as a real camel since it was magic that changed him. The way he rammed the weasel with his chest and drove it into a nearby stand of pine trees made me proud. The medallion flashed all by itself and the weasel disappeared.

Just when everyone started to relax, a fourth weasel jumped from a low-hanging branch in a nearby tree. It was as if a shadow came to life. It would have thrown Kenzie out of the saddle and onto the ground, but the strange, hairy human let out a low yowl and long vines sprang up from the ground, twisting and turning around weasel number four in midair. Even in the dark, I could see long thorns digging into the vicious thing and ripping at its shoulder and neck.

Dusty turned his backside to it and let loose with both hind legs into the glowing red eyes as a luminous orb floated up from the medallion, lighting the whole clearing from above. It flashed and the beast turned to ooze.

"Still up there, Kenzie?" Dusty called out. "Yes," she

squeaked.

"Stay with me," he added.

The hairy human extended its stick toward us with a round glowing globe flashing a silver light. The world around us spun like a ball of yarn across the floor. My stomach felt queasy and Daisy struggled to stay upright. The medallion flashed in return, the silver light twirled back into the globe, and all was right once again.

Dusty's head bobbed up and down as a soft nicker welled out from his throat. The tall, hairy human pulled its stick back and held completely still.

The big guy kept at it, trying to communicate, but I don't think he was getting through. Then something resembling a hairy backpack slid from the back of the creature. No one had noticed it until now. I wondered if the weasels knew about it.

"Can you talk to it?" I asked Dusty.

"I think so, but it's hard to get through, how about you?"

"Let me see?" I opened my mouth. "Meooww."

Kenzie started giggling and it grew to a belly shaking laugh in seconds.

"Meow?" Her body leaned sideways and I thought she might topple from Dusty's back. I don't know what she was laughing about. I did what any good cat always does when approaching strange kittens, I asked if they needed help.

I jumped from the pack saddle and walked over to the pair. They still didn't move, but an odd sense of caring washed over me. I needed to run to them and rub against their legs and then lick their heads. It was the only thing I could focus on.

The smaller one answered back. "Meewoow?"

The little one was twice as tall as Kenzie and he'd been crying. His tummy was empty and he was tired. Little Fuzzy, that was his name, he also said his big sister had a gash in her leg and her whole body ached. I translated for everyone.

"Seriously?" Kenzie asked. "From Meewoow?"

"The little guy's accent was perfect. Cat speak is very efficient." I flicked my tail but doubted Kenzie saw it. "We need to take care of them. The little one is hungry and the big one is hurt." I answered Little Fuzzy back, "*Meoowoor.*"

Dusty blew a breath through his lips that made him sound like he was giving the world a giant raspberry.

"He. The little one is a he," I said. "The big one is a she, older sister."

"I didn't think for a minute these were grown-ups," Dusty said.

"Why not?" Kenzie asked. "The little one, as Kitten calls him, towers over me."

"Mark and I have tracked them in other places. These two are so much shorter than we're used to seeing, and have no scent at all. Grown-ups give off a strong smell." Dusty snorted in a whiff. "You can't miss the smell of an adult Bigfoot."

"Maybe we should take them back to the truck and I could..." Kenzie shifted in the saddle.

"No, we need to take them home." The yellow horse turned to me. "Tell them we want to take them home."

"That won't be necessary," a black bear moaned from up in a tree nearby. It shinnied down and sauntered up the incline behind us.

"Somebody growled again?" Kenzie turned her head from side to side looking for the source of the growl.

"It's just a black bear. Don't worry, it won't hurt us." Dusty scanned all around us. "It looks like we're surrounded by more Bigfoot children too."

"I just noticed too, we're surrounded," I echoed.

"Seriously?" Kenzie swallowed hard. "One good deed and do they show any gratitude?"

"Relax," Dusty replied. "They're not going to hurt us. They've come for their friends."

"Correct," groaned the bear. "You have all passed the test. Liosa has indeed sent you."

CHAPTER 15

The Village of the Bigfoot

The young forest people swarmed Dusty and Daisy like ants on a sugar cube. The kids, if Dusty was to be believed, ranged in height. A few were a little shorter than Kenzie while most were as tall as Dusty. All of them were wide and solid and walked with confident steps. No one stumbled or tripped in the dark, and there wasn't a single one I considered awkward or clumsy. All of them had long and neatly groomed fur that would be the envy of any cat. The youngsters clustered around the horses, touching and stroking their necks as they hummed and clucked their tongues. Kenzie sat as rigid as a tree, holding her breath.

"You understand any of what they're saying?" I asked the big guy.

"Yes," Dusty answered. He gave me a look. Even in the dark I could see a sadness in him that wasn't there before.

"Well?" I asked. "What are they saying?"

"Wait and see. Follow for now." The mob moved forward with Dusty and Daisy. Mark tagged behind.

Little Fuzzy, the youngster Dusty rescued, scooped me up with one arm. This wasn't something I liked, and when I flicked my tail, he had the nerve to scold me in cat language.

"You won't be able to keep up," he said. "Quit your complaining."

The Bigfoot was correct. They moved so fast that I might as well have been sitting in the truck with Kenzie driving us through the moon tunnel. Dusty, Daisy, and Mark strode along at a brisk trot while the mob passed through cluster after cluster of thorny vines. I doubt anything could have followed us without being ripped to shreds.

In spite of the tangle, not a single thorn scratched or poked me or anyone else.

"I call you Little Fuzzy, right?" I asked.

He shushed me with a Bigfoot trill, something like a bird tweet crossed with a purr. These bigfoots, or forest people, passed through brush and briar without a sound. The strangest thing? There were so many of them. How could a group this large trudge through dense, scrubby mountain undergrowth without snapping a twig or breaking a branch?

Dusty's hoof beats—Daisy's, and even Mark's—were the only sound to be heard. This mob didn't strike me as careless in anything they did. I wondered what their parents were like.

The sun peeked up over the horizon to the left as we made our way along the side of a cliff. Sunrise. I looked up at the pale sky and caught sight of the moon sliver still high above. Soon it would start its descent. The bear groaned and ambled off. Several of the children searched along the stone face. Then they pushed their hands inside holes that dotted the rock face.

With a great rumble, a portion of the cliff shifted inward, and we all filed into a wide space.

Dusty's medallion lit up the darkness with soft silver light.

The children hooted, tweeted, whistled, and made a racket.

I guess we didn't need to be quiet anymore.

The children were all over Dusty again, patting and stroking his neck. All the kids seemed to love Dusty. I could tell he loved them back by the big, horsey grin plastered on his mug.

A rumble shook the floor, and the rock wall closed behind us. Another rock face to our right opened. When the shaking stopped, we poured into a brightly-lit cavern with high ceilings. It wasn't bright like daylight but more like a cloudy day without shadows.

Little Fuzzy finally set me down, and Kenzie climbed off Dusty's back.

"Kitten?" Kenzie called. "Stay with me."

Since Kenzie needed comfort and encouragement, I trotted through the ocean of extremely large feet and into Kenzie's arms. Who was I to withhold comfort when it was needed?

We gazed upon a small city of stone buildings and rough-hewn stone paths etched into the floor of the cave. Points of purple light dotted the cavern's ceiling as our hairy escorts led us down the main path and past more stone buildings and wood huts.

We eventually stopped at a large circle with single entrance. It led into an area dotted with trees, flowers, and grass. What greeted us made my tail puff out.

A sandy brown wall rose up before us, nearly as tall as the barn at home and twice as long. Little Fuzzy walked forward to the right side and pointed at a picture of Lisa. She was tall and slender in the picture, young-looking and pale. The image was such a contrast to the image of the wizened old lady, projected from the medallion—but she wore the same dress, so I knew it was her.

Little Fuzzy stepped toward the picture of Lisa and pointed at the one next to it. The next picture was bright and colorful and stretched high up the wall. It displayed all manner of strange figures. Some were human-looking, and others were half this and half that. There were too many creatures in the picture to count at one glance.

Grimalkin was in it too, shown as a little gray kitten hovering in the top left corner.

One figure stood out among them all. It towered high above all of the others, bright as yellow sunlight. My tail felt as if it would pop out every single hair.

Little Fuzzy walked to the middle of the wall and tapped another picture. This one had the big yellow creature fighting the others. In fact, it looked like a war between Lisa and the big, bright creature. In the third picture, the figure was changing color from yellow to gray to black.

"It looks like a fight happened," Kenzie said.

Dusty snorted. His head bobbed up and down.

Fuzzy called for his sister. She limped over and picked him up. He patted another picture, higher up. This one had a six- legged yellow horse with a rider. They were battling an enormous snake five times larger than the truck. A medallion, like the one Lisa had given to Dusty, hung from its saddle. The hairy children crowded around Dusty all over again and patted his shoulder and sides.

"It's like when Dusty visits the sick kids," Kenzie whispered. "The few times I've gone to help, it never fails. Everyone always wants to touch him."

"Rawrwwwww," Mark groaned.

Fuzzy cued his sister to take him to another picture on the far end, passing up others as they moved. This final picture was a big splotch of black, and it was shedding weasels like a— Okay, I'll say it. Magus, the black splotch, was shedding weasels like a cat sheds hair in springtime.

The fifty or sixty Bigfoot children around us busted out wailing and moaning. Fuzzy had only pointed to a few of the pictures. I studied the ones Fuzzy had avoided, especially the last several.

These pictures showed a yellow horse like Dusty

running at the big black splotch. A second picture had a black horse in it that looked like Daisy, standing over a broken stone. The last one was of me, a black cat, sitting upon the body of a yellow horse lying in a circle of red. Kenzie saw it too. Her arms held me tighter as she clenched her jaw.

An alarm went off in my head. Fear spread from my tail all the way to my nose. Kenzie and I couldn't move. If I understood anything about these pictures, it was that most were from the past, but I would bet my whiskers these last three were about the future. This wasn't going to end well.

CHAPTER 16

Surprises

The children led us to a wooden guest hut. It had one large room with several bundles of soft grass against the far wall, and a large stone basin on the other. I smelled water, and so did Dusty and Daisy. They helped themselves to the basin. I really hoped it was a water trough and not like that thing Mark has in bathroom.

"Can you understand the Bigfoots, Kitten?" Kenzie asked. "Only when Little Fuzzy talks cat. How about you, Dusty?"

The big guy's head drooped downwards. Daisy didn't say anything either. Mark found a few vines on one wall and proceeded to chow down, thorns and all. Eeeww.

"What do we do now? Should we pull out the stones and ask them to fix them?" I asked.

"You can try," Dusty said. "They're kids, so I doubt they can fix anything,"

Kenzie unpacked Daisy and brushed her down. Dusty dozed near the water basin, still saddled.

"Do you think we could explore?" Kenzie asked.

Daisy snorted and rumbled a response to us.

"She doesn't think they'll hurt us." Dusty nodded. "Just don't go far. Before you go, Kenzie, could you take my saddle off?"

"What about the medallion?" She asked. "Don't you want to keep it handy?"

Dusty's ears drooped as he let out a sigh. "We'll be fine here without it."

Out on the street, there was no one to be seen. "Where do you think everyone went?"

Kenzie shrugged. "Maybe they went to bed. Let's go back to the pictures. One of them scared me, and I want a closer look."

"You mean..." I looked up at Kenzie and nodded.

"Kitten, I'm not special like you and Dusty. No one has given me some fancy token, but when I saw the picture of you with Dusty lying on the ground..." She shivered. "I don't want to think about the idea of Dusty being hurt, but we can't ignore that...."

"Oh, but you must think about it." Grimalkin's face popped out of nowhere and floated in front of us.

"Ahhhhhh." Kenzie jumped back and then looked down at me. "How does that not scare the..."

"I know who it is. He doesn't frighten me," I said.

Grimalkin's body appeared and lowered to the ground. "Aye, our Sonny Jim there has an aptitude—"

"His name is Kitten," Kenzie corrected the cat. "K-I-T-T- E-N, Kitten."

"Well, you needn't be hateful, Girly. There's a reason I don't always use his name. Names are powerful. Using names improperly complicates things as you are about to learn. But I see you found your way."

"Why are you here?" I asked. "It seems strange that you would be here after Lisa did all the hard work."

"Not at all. I'm here as an impartial observer, and I have a vested interest. My agreement with Lisa must be honored, or it will go hard with me. We guardians take agreements very seriously. When we don't keep our word, we lose bits of our power. The bigger the promise, the more power we lose. Shall we go visit the pictures?"

Grimalkin trotted off toward the murals.

Kenzie shrugged and followed. My tail wasn't tingling, but something wasn't right. This sensation was different from anything I've experienced. It was as if someone was about to step on my tail, and there was no way to avoid it.

Something was going to happen.

We found the gray cat staring up at the cavern ceiling. "Do you notice how bright the cave is?" Grimalkin asked. "It doesn't matter if it's cloudy or sunny outside. As long as it's daylight, the light is fairly good and consistent in here. But when the sun goes down, that's another matter. It's easy for shadows to hide in here then."

"No shadows during the day." Kenzie cast her gaze to the floor. "I think it's the purple-colored pockets all over the ceiling. I bet they're made from feldspar."

"What's that?" I asked.

"A mineral. When it's cut right, it diffuses sunlight." "That's what you were talking about in the barn and my..."

"Your token," Grimalkin interrupted. "You figured it out, sort of." His gaze fastened on the picture of the cat on top of the dying horse. "I trust you've noticed that picture?"

"Why isn't Lisa here?" Kenzie asked. "It's safe enough in the cave."

Grimalkin shook his head. "She needs the moonlight more than ever now, and finds direct sunlight harsh. As weak as she has become these days, she prefers the night side of the earth." He grinned. "Perhaps you've more important things to consider."

The gray cat licked his front paw and wiped his face several times.

"Are the pictures true?" I asked. "There was a horse with six legs in one of the pictures."

Grimalkin stretched and yawned. "The horse, Sleipnir, is the big guy's ancestor and is long gone. Is there something you'd like to ask me straight out, Sonny Jim?"

Kenzie did a little hop. "Yes!"

Grimalkin growled. "Quiet, Girly, this doesn't concern you."

"Yes," I said. "Little Fuzzy walked past three pictures. I was wondering if..."

"If they represent the future? Right? And do they have something to do with you?" Grimalkin trotted closer to the wall. "That depends on whether or not you believe the future is set in stone."

"Is it?" Kenzie asked. "What?" the cat answered. "Set in stone."

"Oh, that. My kind debate this all the time, but it was

Magus who set the course we're on now. We can see bits of the future, but after all this time, we've learned that the future can change once you see it." Grimalkin sat directly beneath the picture of a large figure fighting all the other figures. "Magus was called Primus then, and what you see in the mural was his old form. Once he turned black, a new name was required. He wanted to prove that he did not have to pass on like all of us. Magus wanted to be fully immortal, but his way meant feeding on the life force of others to do so. Somehow he hasn't figured out that once there is no one left to feed on, he will be gone. Magus is trying to live on and it could lead to the ruin of all creation."

"You're saying he's nuts? Crazy?" Kenzie frowned.

"Yes, dearie." The big gray cat blinked.

"So this big fight in the picture happened because Magus was having a temper tantrum?" Kenzie asked. "The guy lives for a long time, if we are to believe you. Shouldn't that be enough?"

"Yes, it should. We do not strictly die but pass on to what my kind eventually must become. He likes what he is now and doesn't want to change, even if it causes ruin. It's driven him insane."

"So all the pictures are true?" I asked. "And how do you know he will cause ruin?"

"Sonny Jim, look at that one painting on the left of the group picture. See the little gray kitten in the picture? The one that hovers above all the rest?"

I flicked my tail.

"I'm pictured up there because I never take sides. I only make agreements when and where it suits me."

Kenzie stood up. "You're not here to help us? You...crook. Double-dealer. Come on, Kitten, we should've known better."

"No," I said, "Wait. What's your game, Grimalkin? Can Magus feed on you if he eats me?"

"You are indeed one of my kits." The gray cat purred. "Magus approached me off and on in what you call the past. He requested my help, but I'm no fool. As unpredictable as I endeavor to be, he is insane and not to be trusted.

"Magus is bonkers?" I hacked up a furball. "Why didn't you off him?"

"We guardians understand all too well how one decision on our part alters so many things.

We always try to never alter the natural course of life. Our first little squabble caused a great deal of damage and harm. Since then, we always use a light touch where all you short-lived creatures are involved. The world must be allowed to unfold as it should, and not influenced by our carelessness."

"That makes no sense. Aren't you interfering now?" Kenzie asked.

Grimalkin blinked a long, slow blink and then yawned. Kenzie turned to leave. "Let's go, Kitten."

"Wait, nothing has changed," I said. "According to that

picture the big guy is going to die."

"That's one way of looking at it." Grimalkin purred and then stretched out on the ground.

"Kenzie, you may not like Grimalkin," I said. "But you like Dusty, right? We're here to save our home. Grimalkin can help us do that." I stood up to stretch, walked over, and rubbed my cheek against her leg. "Come on, don't be discouraged."

"There you go, Boyo," the cat said. "That's thinkin' with your whiskers."

"This is annoying." Kenzie strode away.

I let her walk and turned to Grimalkin. "What was Magus's name again? Before he changed it?"

"Primus," Grimalkin answered. And then the cat vanished. Grimalkin didn't seem like a bad sort to me. He was a cat after all, and we cats don't always answer to someone else's rules. Kenzie was wrong about him—he did want to help. I trotted after Kenzie.

When we returned to the hut and stepped through the door.

Dusty and Daisy were gone.

CHAPTER 17

Betrayal

Dusty?" Kenzie spun around as if our friends could be hiding in the shadows of the hut. "Daisy? ?"

I sniffed the walls and around the water basin. The saddles were still on the floor.

"Mark is gone too." Kenzie rushed out the door and called for the camel. When she came back inside, she said, "This is just fabulous. What is going on?"

"Maybe they went to look around, like us." I moved to the far corner. There my nose picked up a new smell.

Kenzie dashed back outside and called loudly for Mark, Dusty, and Daisy. I was more interested in this new scent. It was familiar.

When Kenzie returned, she leaned against the wall and slid to the floor. "What do we do now? Should we go look for them?" She buried her face in both hands. Water dripped from her eyes.

"I guess a Kitten's work is never done." I ambled over to her and placed my paw on her leg. "Merwoww?"

"Go away."

"Well, you can't blame a cat for trying. It worked before."

"We're all going to die!" she exclaimed.

I sat in her lap and gazed into her face. "What makes you say that?"

"Cats and horses talk, my friend got turned into a camel, and I met Bigfoots or Bigfeets, or whatever you call them. That doesn't even cover the creepy animals with big, sharp claws." She pulled something from her pocket and wiped her nose. "I was brought to a city beneath a mountain by tall, hairy kids where another talking cat insulted me. Dusty, Daisy, and Mark are nowhere to be found. Worst of all, I may never see my home again, Kitten."

"Don't be scared, Kenzie. To me, Kenzie, your name means brave. Did you hear that? Kenzie-brave, Kenzie-trustworthy, Kenzie-compassionate."

"What are you doing?" she asked.

"I use the name weasel because it makes my enemies less formidable. Name magic can work the other way too."

"What does that even mean?" Kenzie stroked my head.

I wished I had brought a few mice with me. I could have given Kenzie one to cheer her up. Her choice, dead or alive. A tasty one would sure cheer me up right now.

"My Da always told us kits that names are like

containers.

They can cause things to leak, but they can become containers for powerful and helpful things. I was filling your name with power." I touched my forehead against hers and nipped the end of her nose. "I'm making you powerful and brave."

Kenzie held me tight. "If Grimalkin set us up, I'm going to strangle him."

"There's a funny smell in that corner." I motioned with my nose. "Jangles used something at home that smelled the same way."

She let me down and then tucked her chin against her chest. I padded over to the saddles and pack. "Kenzie, the medallion was left on the saddle. I can't imagine Dusty going anywhere without it." Kenzie didn't look up.

I pawed at the round piece of metal "I think you should take this off and hang onto it. It shouldn't be left lying around."

"Do I look like your servant?"

I sniffed. "Well, yes, but I'm a cat. Everyone looks like my servant. Even the big guy." I flicked my tail at her and gave her a long, slow blink.

"You sound like Grimalkin." Her mouth scrunched into a little pout. "Where is this Lisa? She could at least appear and help out."

A low thrumming noise vibrated in the air. "Do you hear that?"

Kenzie jumped as if she'd just been grabbed by a weasel. "We're going to die. Kitten, we need to get out of here. We have to get back to the truck."

"What are you talking about?" I asked. "We can't go anywhere yet."

The sound continued. Maybe Kenzie couldn't hear it, but the look on her face told me she felt it. Kenzie trembled and wrapped her arms around herself.

"Well, we can't have this." I trotted to her, and touched her leg with my paw. "Kenzie is brave. Kenzie is powerful. Kenzie. Kenzie. Kenzie." Then I smacked her leg with my claws, not hard, but just enough to make her notice.

"Ow!" She pulled her leg back. "What did you do that for?"

"Get the medallion." She got up, shuffled over to the saddle, and pulled her set of portable claws from her pocket, and scratched at the sticky stuff holding the medallion to the saddle.

I should have been as afraid as Kenzie, but fuzzies, weasels, and the like didn't frighten me. Lisa and Grimalkin called this my aptitude. Besides, living at the ranch had taught me that when you love people, it can make you afraid for them and even act against your own interests on their behalf. You will do things that frighten you just to help them out. The idea of losing my new home and friends made a strange feeling rise from my bones. It was a coldness that made my stomach queasy and made me want to run away. But I wouldn't. Dusty, Daisy, and Mark needed me. Besides, the big guy would never stand around and do nothing, even if he were afraid.

"Dusty and Daisy are in trouble, and so is the camel," I said. "They need us. I know you care for them too much to abandon them now."

Kenzie mumbled something, so I gave her another swipe on the hip.

"Ow! Stop that!"

"Come on," I said. "There's a steady noise you can't hear.

It may be what's making you feel afraid."

"So you're not afraid?" Kenzie asked.

"No, not of the noise. But there are other things that bother me. Like the idea of Magus wiping out tuna forever and forever."

Kenzie tucked the medallion in her pocket. "Now what?"

"Out the door and to your right."

"I want to go the other way," she protested.

I raised my paw like I might swat her. "To the right."

She shuffled out the door and down the stone street with me on her heels as if I were some kind of herding dog. How demeaning. But what could I do? She couldn't be left on her own, and I needed her pockets and thumbs.

Kenzie wobbled on her feet. "Oh, Kitten, let's turn back." Kenzie's gaze darted back and forth as if she were ready to bolt.

"Keep going, we're close. Kenzie, Kenzie, Kenzie."

We'd gone down the street for several minutes, and Kenzie's whole body trembled as she struggled to stay on her feet. Thankfully, we didn't need to go far. We stopped at a stone hut this time.

"Sit out here," I said.

I almost had to scratch her again. Her gaze shot down the street. After a few seconds, she slid down the wall and sat.

I stepped into her lap and touched my nose against hers.

"You will be fine. Kenzie is brave."

"If you say so, Kitten. Be careful." She kissed my head.

There were no doors on any of these places, so entering was easy. That was a good thing because my nose had already found that smell again. The low-pitched sound grew louder.

Little Fuzzy lay on the floor, his hands and feet bound with some sort of vine.

"*Meowwwrrrrrrrow*," he said.

"Hush now," I scolded. "Don't be afraid. Kenzie and I are here, but you must stop that wailing because it upsets Kenzie."

He stopped for a second but almost burst into another round of sobs. I swatted him good and hard on the nose, without any claws.

Little Fuzzy sucked in a breath.

I got a close look at his face now. His nose was thick

and flat. His eyes were set wide apart and had a gold tinge to them. He also sported a short pair of fangs. And he wore a glowing symbol in the shape of a cat face below his eye.

Grimalkin's brood?

"Listen up, Kenzie has a portable set of claws that she can cut you free with. But you must stop upsetting her. We need her to come in and help."

Little Fuzzy sniffed and went silent. A scent rolled off this youngling like the odor in the guest house we had just been in. It made me feel happy.

"Kenzie, please come inside," I called.

No answer.

I walked to the doorway, thinking she might have run off, but there she was, staring up at the roof of the cavern.

"If I could get some of those stones from there, I bet I could make a wentzel— Sorry...a weasel gun." She looked down at me and smiled.

"That was a quick change."

"From what? What are you talking about?" she asked.

"Nothing. Sounds like a good idea. Could you bring your portable claws and help Little Fuzzy get untied?"

"Sure."

This was the normal Kenzie, the one who wasn't afraid of anything. Kenzie, Kenzie, Kenzie.

"Why are we here? Weren't we back in the other hut? Did we find everyone? I do remember you swatting me, twice." Kenzie flashed me a cross look.

"Later," I said.

Kenzie pulled her claws out and sawed at Little Fuzzy's bindings. "Don't move."

I was about to translate when Little Fuzzy responded, "Thank-ooh, Ken'-zee."

"Well, that was unexpected," I said.

Little Fuzzy flashed his fangs at the girl, and she jumped back, nearly slicing into his wrist.

"He's smiling at you."

Kenzie blinked. "Oh." She pressed her lips together and let a smile slowly reach across her face. Fuzzy matched it immediately. "Wow, you're smart," Kenzie said.

This time Fuzzy's smile was genuine and natural.

"He's like me and Dusty," I said. "He understands everyone."

"What happened?" I asked the Bigfoot. "Where's Dusty?"

Fuzzy went into a tirade of groans, trills, burps, and sounds I'd never heard before.

"Slow down." Kenzie cut off the last of Fuzzy's bonds. "Kitten and I can't understand you if you talk too fast."

"I wish he had a tail. He could say so much in far less time."

"Matpas and Fatpas were taken," Fuzzy said.

"By Magus?" I responded.

Fuzzy nodded. "Magus."

"What are Matpas and Fatpas?" Kenzie folded her knife up.

I looked up at Kenzie. "Mothers and Fathers."

"We should have another name for Magus." Kenzie made her way around the room. "Maggot. That was Dusty's idea."

Fuzzy went quiet and studied us. His eyes went wide and he showed his fangs as he attempted something I took as a laugh.

"Maggot," he said. "Maggot taked them and put in dark cave. He say we do what told or—" The little

Bigfoot's expression stretched to a frown, and I was certain he might start wailing again.

"We understand," I said. "We say *held hostage.*"

"Every night since Maggot come, we go out and he send weasels to hunt us, hurt us, but never kill us. He want to catch moon horse. When moon horse show up and defeat weasels, we tell horse everything right away. We not lie."

"Hold on." Kenzie crossed her arms. "You mean you told Dusty the truth?"

"We love moon horse. Many have come before him. We not want this one to die, but his purpose to protect. He tell us he come and help, but wait until you..."

"Leave," I said, my eyebrows scrunching down. "The Grass Bag has a plan that excludes me. Of all the nerve."

"Dusty is officially in trouble now," Kenzie said. "Wait until I get my hands on him."

"I change mind," Fuzzy said. "Before they take him to Maggot. It not right for moon horse to die for us. I cry and make fuss, and they all start to..."

"Freak out?" Kenzie nodded.

"They tie me up, so I not follow."

"Dusty knew." I traded gazes with Kenzie. Of all the pig- headed things to do. "I figured something was wrong when I asked him. He understood the kits right away, and he lied to me."

"Why would he do that? We have to do something," Kenzie said. "I wish we had a weasel gun."

Fuzzy pulled out a round glass circle from somewhere beneath his fur.

"Oh, dude!" I didn't even want to think where that thing had been.

Kenzie's expression shifted to a grimace. Yep, she didn't want to think too hard about it either.

"You need this." He passed it off to Kenzie, who managed to hold it between her thumb and finger. I was just glad I didn't have to take it in my mouth.

"Mootpah use to make...toes?

"Mootpah?" Kenzie winced.

"I think that's like a grandparent," I said.

"Toes?" Kenzie asked.

Fuzzy scrunched his eyebrows at me.

"Tones?"

"Tokens?" Kenzie asked.

Fuzzy smiled. "To-kens."

"Can you make them?" Kenzie asked.

He shook his head. "Not good as Mootpah."

"Great," Kenzie huffed.

"What about your little light?" I looked up at Kenzie.

"Remember my token and what we did with the beasel?"

Kenzie pulled out the little light stick from her pocket and held the round disk up to the lamp. "This is a tactical flashlight like the Navy SEALS use. Nineteen dollars online with free shipping."

I sniffed it.

"It's got five settings, and it's capable of eleven hundred lumens." Kenzie held it out for us to see.

I stared and Fuzzy wrinkled his nose.

"What's a lumen?" I asked.

"Right, never mind." Kenzie took the disk and held it to the front of her light and flipped the switch on.

The light spread everywhere and took on a purple color.

"Is it broke?" I asked.

"My sparkly made all kinds of patterns and..."

"It enough, even for Maggot. Only Mootpah and Footpah make better ones."

"I have to get the duct tape from the pack and a short stick." Kenzie pulled out Lisa's medallion from her pocket. "Would this work too?"

Fuzzy took it from Kenzie and shook his head. "No, not work same way. Mootpah made that. It for something different. It a seed."

"Seed?" I asked.

"Kit-ten, you help moon horse?" he asked.

"Duh."

"Don't be rude, Kitten," Kenzie said. "We both will."

"Then I take you to place so you get help. Okeydokey?" Kenzie snickered.

"I didn't teach him that, did you?" I gazed up at Kenzie.

"No," Kenzie replied. "Have you ever heard me say that?"

CHAPTER 18

Mootpah's Shop

We stopped back at the empty hut before leaving, where we had left the pack saddle. Kenzie pulled out a smaller pack and loaded it with rope and other useful things. She also included cat treats. Kenzie had such potential.

"Mark always brings a gun with him," Kenzie said. "At home, it's locked in a safe, but I didn't know the combination."

"Forest people know about guns. Gun not work against weasel," Fuzzy pointed at the pocket where Kenzie had stored the flashlight. "Only thing."

"Kitten, did you teach him to use weasel and..." Kenzie pushed matches and something she called jerky into the small pack and closed it. It smelled awesome!

"No, but I think Fuzzy may be one of Grimalkin's heroes.

Fuzzy's real big on that name stuff, and he has a mark." Kenzie slung the pack onto her back. "Let's go."

Fuzzy took us to a cave, but I have to say, following him was like trying to catch Kenzie driving the old beater truck in the pasture. We weren't more than four or five houses from the place where we found Fuzzy, and we had already lost sight of him. Eight times, Fuzzy came back and found us every time.

"You slow," he said.

"Duh," Kenzie replied. "Compared to you, yes."

Without a word, he seized Kenzie and hefted her over his shoulder. He didn't even give me a look, "You run now."

Fuzzy took off.

He paced past larger buildings, and I lost him five more times. Oh, and I was running too. That meant I was focusing on catching up with him rather than paying attention to where I was going. Where are the tree branches and old forests when you need them?

I finally caught up with Fuzzy and Kenzie, but only because they stopped to get a drink of water. They were sitting at a little spring bubbling out from a cluster of rocks. I had to sit down.

Fuzzy shook his hairy head. "You really slow."

"My legs are shorter than yours."

Kenzie pulled out a cup from the pack and filled it with water for me.

"Thank you."

"I take you to sacred place. No one but forest people ever see. Mootpah's work place."

At least they let me catch my breath and get a drink of water before Fuzzy led us through a wide crack in a cliff wall, and down a narrow path between boulders. We eventually came to a dead end.

Fuzzy stopped at a solid wall of rock. "Follow me." Kenzie gave me a wide-eyed stare. "What do we do now?"

"I have no idea," I answered back.

Fuzzy grinned.

Kenzie wrapped her arms around her chest and bobbed up and down on her tiptoes. She was nervous, and so was I.

"Wait a minute," I sniffed at the wall. It didn't smell like anything. Usually, things like mud, bug juice, and pollen collect on rock walls. There was no scent whatsoever. My eyes told me the wall was there, but my nose said otherwise.

I raised my paw and pushed against the rock. It passed through.

"It's okay, Kenzie, see?" I shoved my paw through again.

"You coming?" Fuzzy disappeared through the wall. I jumped high into the air and scampered for cover.

"You jumpy, Kit-ten." Fuzzy poked his head out through wall. "Hurry up. Not much time." Fuzzy shook his head and pulled it back through the stone.

Kenzie tried to touch the rock face. "It's like a hologram. Maybe this isn't so scary after all." She scooped me up. "Here goes nothing."

CHAPTER 19

Revelations

Wow." Kenzie's pupils expanded, but then shrank at the bright daylight from those strange purple rocks. Other parts of the cave glowed with fire-toned orange crystals. Work benches lay where they had fallen, along with stacks of tools, rags, boxes, and a couple of things that might have been chairs. At the far end was a well-ordered display of rocks. These had clear surfaces, with the weird squiggly lines that made my tail tingle. Moonstones. Ours was broken now, and its fate entered my mind as I surveyed the mess. Wow—this place had been hit by a tornado.

Boom. Crash.

As soon as my feet touched solid ground, I scattered for cover. Every bit of my fur was standing on end, except for the fur on my tail. Go figure. I think that meant nothing magical was going to eat me for breakfast. That only left non-magical things wanting me for their mid-morning snack.

There was an open spot beneath a short table that fit me just fine while Kenzie managed to climb up on top.

"You scaredy cat, Kitten." Fuzzy chirped, making his body quiver. "You much braver around weasels than little bits of noise."

"Grimalkin says I have an aptitude for weasels, but I still startle."

Kenzie jumped down and pulled the pieces of our token from her pack, showing them to Fuzzy. Her eyes held a wicked glare that could melt glass. "Can you fix this or not?"

He grabbed the pieces and pitched them over his shoulder.

Clink!

They landed on the rock floor. "Even Mootpah can't fix." Kenzie's chin drooped. She sighed and slapped her thighs.

"All this for nothing?"

Fuzzy tilted his long, hairy face and scrunched his flat nose, making it almost disappear in an ocean of wrinkles and fur. Slowly the corners of his mouth spread wider, revealing a gorgeous set of fangs, white and very clean.

Kenzie cringed.

"Me no say that. Me allowed to help. That why you here.

You need new, but you learn thing first."

Fuzzy fiddled with a box of tools sitting on the top of a nearby bench. He must not have found what he was looking for because he scurried off to other benches, picking and scavenging through the piles of tools and multiple boxes littering the place.

Kenzie was drawn to a white screen next to us. She held her fist before it with two fingers sticking up and bounced it up and down. I could just catch her singing something about some bunny named Foo Foo.

Fuzzy raced back and blocked her arm. "No do. Bad."

Kenzie jerked away from him. "What's so bad about bunny shadows? Besides, your Mootpah uses soft light in here. I don't think I could raise a shadow if I tried."

"First thing Mootpah teach. Shadow only hole in light. If hole fill with bad things, you get weasels and Maggots. If hole not filled, Lisa and cat-thing trip over shadow skeletons. Get mad. When you hold fist near screen, you make Kenzie-fist- sized hole in light."

"That's just stupid," Kenzie huffed. "Soft light doesn't work that way. We used it to take down a beasel back home. Hit it right in the eye."

"Soft light?" Fuzzy inquired. "Beasel?"

"New kind of weasel. Bigger than Dusty," I added. "Soft light is what Kenzie calls light filtered through objects. It doesn't make shadows."

Fuzzy pulled another creepy face for us, but I'm sure he was just thinking hard. "What you call soft light make door to different place. You send beasel...somewhere."

"My mom works with lights and pictures all the time." Kenzie pulled out her makeshift weasel gun. "You diffuse light by shining it through something that spreads it out so it can't create shadows. Like the feldspar lens you gave me, you know, the purple stones in the cavern ceiling."

Fuzzy resumed rummaging through various piles of boxes scattered about the shop.

"No," he said. "Wrong."

Kenzie raised her fist again, but I glared at her. She lowered her hand.

"What?" Kenzie huffed. "We don't have time for this."

"Found it," Fuzzy said, and trotted back to us.

"Mootpah's ceiling crystals make gateway. Sends shadow to other places. That why we safe in cavern during the day. Night has different problems. When shades and weasels try to get in here in daylight, they sent other place."

"Shades?" I asked.

"Shadows filled with bad things. Shades." Fuzzy reached for another box.

Kenzie put her hands on her hips. "Even if that were true, where do they go?"

Fuzzy shrugged. "Depend. Your stone, when work, only send shadows away, do nothing more. Symbols on stone give address where things sent. Can't tell where your stone sent them. Too broke."

I flicked my tail. "Me and the big guy have done our share of weasel busting in the pasture. When we drove them into the ground, which was protected by our token, they seemed to melt more than disappear."

"Whatever," Kenzie said. "How does this help us?"

"Well," I purred. "The idea of sending weasels away does seem helpful."

"You facing Magu—" Fuzzy clamped a large hand over his mouth and completely covered his face. Probably because he didn't want to say Maggot's name.

"No worries," I said. "Dusty calls him Maggot."

Fuzzy's whole body shook again. "Good one, funny.

Maggot not problem." Lowering his voice, Fuzzy spelled out the word "P-R-I-M-U-S. He problem."

"Are you talking about that big shiny thing in the pictures?" I asked. "Don't tell me we got to come up with another name?"

"He not shiny anymore." Fuzzy nodded and held up a small cloth bag and a mallet. He handed the bag to Kenzie.

"Hold bag. When I say open, open and close quick. Make sure mouth of bag point up."

Kenzie rolled her eyes and took the bag. "Can we go now?"

He held the mallet above the bag. "Open and close."

A beam of sunlight lazed upward from the bag, immersing the mallet before it hit the ceiling. Still, there was no shadow. Kenzie, following directions, closed the bag almost instantaneously as Fuzzy looked around and grinned.

"See?" Kenzie said. "No shadow. Hey, Fuzzy, can you say *soft light*?"

Fuzzy stretched out his long arm and pointed at a screen at the far end of the shop. A section of it was bathed in orange-toned light; a large mallet-shaped shadow stretched across it.

"How did that happen? That's impossible!" Kenzie exclaimed.

Fuzzy pulled a long, colorless crystal off his body from what I can only hope was a hidden pouch or belt, shook it, and put it back. A narrow corridor of orange light appeared, connecting us and the screen.

"Watch, Kenzie."

The shadow mallet peeled off the screen and floated through the orange light toward us. Fuzzy waved his hand to the right and into soft light. The shadow mallet jumped out of the corridor and appeared back on the screen.

"See?" Fuzzy smirked. "Mootpah's crystals direct shadows and make them go places using different kinds of "soft light.""

"Spectrum," Kenzie said. "Light has different spectrums. Some are seen, other times it can refer to the intensity of light versus its wavelength.

Fuzzy cocked his and gave Kenzie a look like the ones I get from mice as I'm about to grab them with my claws.

Fuzzy shook the look from his face. "Stones with certain markings send shadows to same place. Making your own shadows that can do things takes lots of practice, no time for you to learn. That why I gave you purple lens for Kenzie's con-trap- tion. Purple cause less problems."

"Problems?" I asked. "How does this help us, and just what do you mean by *problems*?"

Fuzzy pulled out the crystal again, shook it, but set it on a table this time. Someone needs to get that boy a purse, or something. He beckoned the shadow again and it peeled off the screen. This time, it went to one of the nearby benches covered in actual sunlight. Where the light came from, I had no idea. He pounded his fist in the air, and the shadow mallet smashed the table to scrap wood. Kenzie jumped. Me, I was back under my table.

"Shadow not just hole in light. Shadow become a skin you can fill with things. You fill with bad, it do bad. You not fill, it make harmless bunny shadows on wall. Fill with good. Nice things can happen. Shadow only how you make it."

"So, your kind of shadows are more like a container or jar," Kenzie added. "So is that what Mag—" She clamped a hand over her mouth. "Is Maggot a container of bad intentions?"

Fuzzy scrunched his face again and let out a trill. "Keep watching."

He picked up the mallet and pounded another table top. It didn't break the table, it only made noise. I made my way back, but another loud crash sent me beneath the table one more time. After wiggling back out, I watched the mallet's shadow move in the same motion of the real mallet and destroy another bench. Fuzzy took up an orange crystal from a nearby shelf. It was a round lens about twice the size of one of Dusty's eyes.

"Weasel gun, please." He reached toward Kenzie.

She drew back and wrapped her arms around the pack.

"Kenzie," I said, as I shimmied back from beneath the table yet again. "Give him your weasel gun."

"It's my good flashlight. I just got it."

"Meow." I gave her my pathetic look. The one that makes Mark give me tuna.

"Only if you quit dodging under that table every time there's a loud noise."

Kenzie pulled out her weasel gun and pointed it at the shadow mallet on the screen. She flicked the switch on her flashlight and sent a beam of white light shooting through the purple crystal. It disappeared, but when she turned it off, it reappeared back on the screen at the other end of the room. "I didn't kill it? It only moved temporarily?"

Fuzzy grabbed the weasel gun.

"Hey." She reached to grab it back, but Fuzzy just stepped away from her reach.

He rummaged through yet another box and pulled a bunch of pieces from it. In seconds, he assembled something resembling Kenzie's weasel gun, slapped the orange lens in it, and attached Kenzie's flashlight. This weasel gun was a much sturdier version than the one Kenzie made. I looked up at Kenzie.

"What?" she said. "If I had access to a shop and extra parts I could have made mine look this cool."

Kenzie gritted her teeth and flashed me the stink eye as she crossed her arms. She'd been hanging around Dusty too long.

Within minutes the thing was done and Fuzzy handed it back to Kenzie. He pointed to his mallet. "Shoot mallet."

Kenzie did. All that happened was that the mallet got a nice dose of orange light.

He set the mallet down on a table much farther away from us. Then he pointed. "Shoot shadow on screen."

Kenzie aimed. Light burst forth from the flashlight and through the orange lens, hitting the shadow mallet. In less time than it takes for me to flick my tail, the shadow vanished and the mallet exploded into a cloud of sawdust. My nose burst into a series of sneezes.

"Weasel burgers." Kenzie grinned.

"Sending shadow away not solve problem," Fuzzy said. "Shadow magic mean pour self into shadow. Shadow alive, but not problem. Problem what make shadow. The forest people can make, but don't. Guardians can make, and some heroes do it. Can't hurt shadow it only con...tain...ner. You must deal with maker of shadow. Stop maker, stop shadows."

"That's lame." Kenzie crossed her arms and slouched. "How come Lisa gave Mark something that only sends shadows away? It did nothing to solve problems. They only come back."

"Lisa not want to kill," Fuzzy said.

Kenzie raised her eyebrow at Fuzzy. "So, if I shine the light from the new weasel gun directly on someone, it doesn't hurt them, right?"

Fuzzy nodded.

"If I hit a shadow from someone making shadow magic," Kenzie continued, "it can blow them up?"

Fuzzy flashed those big fangs of his in a smile. "It why Lisa give you shadow-mover only. No one get hurt."

I jumped up on the nearest bench. "I guess that makes sense."

Fuzzy added, "Weasel gun not tell difference between bad or good. Lisa not want innocent people or animals get hurt. Think about animals and people whose shadow might hit the ground. It hurt Mark, Dusty, Daisy, Kitten, everyone. That why you only borrow new weasel gun."

Kenzie scowled. "I'm getting my flashlight back, right?"

"Aww." Fuzzy scraped the cavern floor with his foot. "I like flashlight."

"Fuzzy." I flicked my tail at him for emphasis.

The bigfoot child rolled his eyes. "All right. You get back." He grabbed another mallet off a different table. He pointed at its shadow on the wall. "Shadow, or shade, is Maggot." Then he let out a trill and several strange noises. He pointed at the real mallet. "P–R–I–M–U–S real problem, not shadow."

"And weasels?" I asked.

"Weasels similar, but not same. Gun get them too, for most part."

"You understand everything the Bigfoot said?" Kenzie asked. "All we need to do is shoot Maggot, but not...? We need to give him another name."

"Yes, I understand him completely. I'm not as fast as Dusty at this communicating stuff, but don't tell him. You are also right, we need to come up with another name."

Fuzzy pursed his lips and wrung his hands. "We have name." The bigfoot opened his mouth and yodeled for twenty seconds.

Kenzie burst out laughing, but then went silent. "I can't say that."

Something occurred to me, Fuzzy wasn't telling us everything. "All right, Fuzzy, I think you left something out."

"P–R–I–M–U–S old and powerful. Big bag of light. Might have to shoot Maggot much. Weasel gun not work in complete dark either. To sus-st-ain shadow enough to hit you will need light."

"So, if I wanted to use the new weasel gun, and it's so dark we couldn't see a shadow, it wouldn't do us any good. There needs to be enough light, hard light, to sustain shadows. Can this get any more complicated?" Kenzie packed the weasel gun away.

When Fuzzy turned his back, I jumped on the other table and pushed the bag of light off the bench and onto the floor. Hey, it's a cat thing.

Kenzie didn't miss a thing. She bent down and palmed the little bag while pretending to tie her shoe.

"Now that wasn't so difficult, was it?" Grimalkin walked up to us, but not in the usual way with his face and body appearing from thin air. The old gray cat walked straight through the wall. "I'm not as fond of this room as were the rest of my kind. Do they have all they need, Fuzzy?"

Fuzzy nodded and then bowed.

"The obligation of the Bigfoot is met." Grimalkin flicked his tail.

"We haven't heard everything Fuzzy has to say on the matter."

"No time. Now what have you children learned?" the gray cat asked.

"Dusty's in trouble, and you want to give us a quiz?" Kenzie cast her hands upward. "Seriously?"

"We have to deal directly with Pr—" I huffed. "We need to think of a different name for him."

"Primate," Kenzie volunteered.

"What's that?" I asked.

"It's another word for monkey." Kenzie grinned.

"Monkey Boy," I said with an arch of my back. Kenzie smiled and stroked my back.

"Are you quite done, children?" Grimalkin scowled, but his lips twitched.

"We flash the new weasel gun directly on the Maggot, the shadow of Monkey Boy."

"Primate? Monkey Boy? It has such an irreverent ring to it. I like it. Now remember," Grimalkin went on, "you must hold the light steady on his shadow to really make an impact. For how long? That's anyone's guess. He is very old."

"What if his shadow disappears? The new weasel gun only works with shadows present."

"You'll just have to figure something out, won't you?" Grimalkin said.

"That's just great." I flicked my tail back at him

"You all did want to try this. Daisy and Dusty could have gone with me. Maggot would probably have left you alone."

"And Mark would be stuck as a camel," Kenzie added.

Grimalkin flicked his tail again. A low growl vibrated in his throat. Time to change the subject.

"According to Fuzzy," I said. "I'm thinking this will also deal with weasels and any other shadow constructs."

Kenzie sighed and patted the pack where the gun had been put away.

"Close enough." Grimalkin purred.

"That means this will work?" I asked.

"Let's hope so," Grimalkin answered. "Kitten and Kenzie, you are kits after me own heart."

"Hope?" My heart skipped a beat. That didn't sound very definite. "Where is Monkey Boy? Not Maggot, but the original?"

Grimalkin answered my question with a question. "If Lisa is where the moon light always shines, where would he be?"

"Where there's hard light." Kenzie patted her pack again.

"Wrong," Grimalkin said. "He would be where no one could hurt his shadow. Consider the bag of light Fuzzy used. In dark places, even the smallest of light can be powerful. Think of Primus as a bag of light, self-contained with the very primal energy consumed from many of us guardians. Since he's been busy consuming the rest of us, he's become rather self- contained. As frightening as his shadow is, when he uses it, he's vulnerable." Grimalkin rubbed his cheek against Kenzie's leg. "You've got talent, there's no denying it. Now I have a reward for you. There's a tunnel that connects this place to Mootpah's safe room."

CHAPTER 20

Mootpah

One moment we were talking to Grimalkin. The next moment, he disappeared. Fuzzy's eyes widened.

"Where did he go?" Kenzie asked.

Fuzzy set off for the door.

"Follow him," I said.

Fuzzy disappeared right through it.

"Hologram," Kenzie said.

"I hear another sound, but I can barely make it out. It's similar to the low-frequency sounds that freaked you out earlier."

Kenzie rolled her eyes at me. "Yeah, right."

We stepped through the fake wall, but something or someone grabbed me. An enormous hand wrapped around me, and I was trapped in a big fist. I bit and clawed at it. The thing had all the taste of a shade.

It didn't let go.

I remembered the shadow mallet—biting it was useless.

Kenzie yelled and screeched. Still nothing from Fuzzy. The sounds of struggle echoed all around us. We had to be inside a tunnel, but that didn't stop our attackers from moving us along. We'd been caught by shadows.

"Kenzie!" I shouted. "Use the weasel gun."

My captor sent me flying through a wall, but I still managed to land on my feet. Kenzie wasn't as graceful. She landed on me.

"That's right, squash the little black kitty cat. Get-off-of- me."

"I'm sorry, Kitten."

The sound of a low-pitched snickering echoed all around us, and when Kenzie finally moved, we found ourselves in a hut. For all I knew, it could have been the one we started out in. "Where's Fuzzy?" Kenzie asked. "And where are we now?"

"Think of this as a temporary office," a deep voice said.

I looked for shadows and noticed my tail hadn't puffed out. "Well, it would seem Grimalkin has kept his word to the letter," the voice said. "Now I must keep mine." "Show yourself," I said.

"I think not," the voice answered. "Call me Mootpah. As you can tell, my kind have become very good at manipulating shadow and light. You are here because

Primus made an agreement with me. He would let my forest people go and never trouble us again if we helped him catch the moon horse. On behalf of my people, I agreed. I also must apologize for the deception."

"You set Dusty up?" I asked. "He's never done anything to you."

"Young cat, Primus and his Magus have troubled us since he and his kind started their squabble eons ago. He stole our shadow magic and has used it to further his own ends. He has even used it against us. This was the easiest way to be rid of him once and for all with the least amount of life being lost."

"That stinks," Kenzie said. "You're going to allow Dusty to be killed?"

"Little human, Dusty offered his life voluntarily, but all is not lost. I also made an agreement with Grimalkin. Allowing my Kitcah to help you and show you what you need to know to defeat Primus was a part of that."

Kenzie glared at me. "You said his name was Fuzzy."

"Kitcah means grandchild," I said. "And that's not the point."

"Poor Dusty." Kenzie shook her head.

"Exactly." I flicked my tail.

"The moon horse agreed to this. We did not force him, nor would we. This is not our way," Mootpah said. "The children explained our problems with Magus after Dusty proved himself capable. The moon horse is tender-hearted and compassionate. Liosa chose well."

"When did he do this?" I asked. "He never—"

"He didn't tell us," Kenzie said. "He understood them all along, and he didn't tell us."

"I wouldn't be too hard on him. Dusty was concerned about your reaction. He said you would defend him and get yourselves hurt. He didn't want that. The death of someone named Jangles weighed heavily upon him."

A section of the wall shimmered. A shimmer the size of Fuzzy moved past us. "My Kitcah was helpful. He showed you everything you need to know. Farewell."

"Wait!" Kenzie held out her hands. "Are we dealing with Maggot or Monkey Boy?"

Mootpah laughed. "Yes—Maggot, that's very good. And useful. I think Monkey Boy is my favorite. They are one and the same, but can you tell me what a shadow is?"

"It is a dark area on a surface that happens when a solid

object comes between light and a surface."

Trust Kenzie to sound like a Google search.

"It's more like a hole in the light," Mootpah said. "It can store all manner of things if you know how to project your essence into it. The shadow is not the object, the essence that can fill it makes an object. Soft light, as you call it, has its uses. Ultimately you must defeat the object casting the shadow if you wish to succeed."

"What are you going to do with us?" I asked.

"Nothing," Mootpah responded. "I made no such agreement with Primus, or Magus, to get in your way. You are free to go, but I'm sure someone is going to need your help very soon. The guardians have the ability of foresight. They can look at all future possibilities. They are difficult to trick. That was why Liosa thought of you, Kitten. Once you attracted her attention, you attracted Primus's. Dusty will need your assistance."

"You mean Monkey Boy," Kenzie said.

Mootpah's laughter bellowed through the office. "I have cleared the forest people from our city so no one will be hurt, or get in your way. Your friends desperately need your assistance."

A black circle formed in front of us. Mootpah's voice started to fade. "Shadows can be portals to other places, but only if you know how to use them. This one will put you in a safe place close to Dusty, but hurry, oblivion is closing in on him."

CHAPTER 21

Monkey Boy and Moron

Mootpah was right. We stepped through the shadow and into a dark hole. It's a good thing I don't need lots of light in order to see in the dark, because there were no fancy stones to give off soft, hard, or plain old light.

"Where are we?" Kenzie reached down with her paw and touched my back.

All I could see were rocky walls. "How am I supposed to know?"

"You're a hero. Besides, you always act like you know everything. At least Dusty is polite about it. You're also a cat and can see in the dark."

Of course, Kenzie didn't know I saw her stick her tongue out at me.

"*Rrwwrrooooowrrr.*"

"That's Mark," I said. "Good ol' Mark, giving us a direction. Coming?"

"I can't see." Kenzie groped around and found my tail. "I need to hold your tail."

Great shades of tuna, the things I put up with because humans have movable thumbs.

"You better not pull it," I warned.

"Then don't get us lost," she answered.

"*Rrwwrrooooowrrr.*"

I could finally understand Mark. It was hard, but camel breath was starting to make sense. He was calling for me. How in the world Dusty understood everyone so quickly was beyond me.

"*Rrwwrrooooowrrr.*"

"We need to hurry," I said. "You know; you could pull out your new weasel gun. It does make a nice light."

"Just one part of it, but Fuzzy fastened it down. I don't think I can take it off. Don't we want to be stealthy?" Kenzie asked. "We don't want to tip off Monkey Boy."

"*Rrwwrrooooowrrr.*"

"Mark says Dusty isn't well."

My excellent eyesight found a path in seconds, and after a few turns, we discovered a faint pink glow pulsing out from a small cave.

"Kenzie, get your gun."

"Wow, you're as bossy as Dusty."

We crept along a narrow rocky path until we came to the opening. A cavern the size of our corral opened up before us. Soft pink light shone from something attached to the ceiling the size of a basketball bathing the whole cavern. No shadows anywhere. Voices echoed toward us, especially Mark's camel calls.

A small, stocky figure came into view near the back wall. This must be Primus. Before him, Dusty was chained to the ground.

"*Rrwwrrooooowrrr.*"

I motioned with my tail for Kenzie to take cover behind a large rock near the entrance. To my surprise, Kenzie did as she was told.

She crept along the wall and took her position. I could hear her pulling the weasel gun from the pack.

"*Rowrrrrrrrr.*"

"Why did I turn him into a camel?" Primus muttered to himself. "By the way—hello, Kitten and Kenzie. Welcome to the end of your world."

The pink light grew brighter, and wouldn't you know it, still no shadows.

Primus—sorry—Monkey Boy didn't look anything like the mural. The top of his head would have come to Kenzie's chest if he were to stand on a box next to her. His upper body was muscled, and his head was completely bald.

"Dude, you look nothing like your picture," I said.

"Camels are so obnoxious," he muttered. "That's the last time I ever borrow that bridle from the Moss Witch. She assured me the human would turn into a horse."

A long groan vibrated from inside the cavern. It was Dusty. Poor Dusty. He was lying down, anchored to the ground with shadow chains. His breathing was shallow, and I could see cuts and gashes, even smell some of them still oozing. Images of what Maggot had done to Jangles only the night before played in my head.

"What's the matter, Dusty?" Primus asked. "You've been so chatty with all the little forest people and that mangy cat friend of yours. Nothing to say? No greetings?"

Primus clenched his fist and the pink light grew brighter still. Dusty laid on his back chained to a big spot on the ground, just like in the mural. The only thing needed to complete the portrait was for me to join the party and sit on him.

"Kenzie," I flicked my tail, taking a chance I could make her understand. "Stay out of sight but be ready."

"You kept your bargain and let the forest people go. Right, Monkey Boy?" I approached Dusty, my tail completely puffed out. This was full-tail alert. "Mootpah told us about it. Don't you Lisa-types work that way?"

Primus tottered a bit, but I wasn't sure what caused it. Calling him Monkey Boy? I had only used the name once and it seemed to have an instant effect. I joined Dusty, but refused to sit on him, like in the picture.

"If the younglings caught the moon horse for you, you would leave them all alone. That was your agreement?"

"Oh, yes. And I will never trouble them again. My kind tend to lose power when we break our word. We're old-school in that way."

Dusty's form grew bright yellow and then faded, like he was pulsing light. I reached a paw to touch him. Was he dying? I thought of the mallet in the workshop and what happened when we hit its shadow. There were no shadows in here, just that strange pink light. I wondered if the moon horse was being drained.

"Aren't you adorable." Primus said. "Were you the best Liosa could send?"

"Somehow, I thought you'd be taller," I purred. "I didn't know what to call you, so we gave you a new name. Your real name sounds a lot like primate, or monkey. So, we all agreed to call you Monkey Boy. It has a real ring to it, doesn't it?"

Primus shuddered a bit and stumbled. He managed a weak grin as he steadied himself.

Dusty stirred. His eyes opened, and he flicked his ears at me. "Kitten."

"You ought to be ashamed of yourself," I answered back with my tail. "I leave you alone for two minutes, and here you are, being lazy. Why did you lie? You told Kenzie not to lie to her parents."

"I didn't lie, not really. I just didn't tell you everything. I couldn't bear the thought of anyone else getting hurt because of me."

Primus laughed. "Well, aren't you the cute couple? With you around to brighten his spirits, Kitten, Dusty might even make it to tomorrow night. Which is what I really need. He needs to last until just before the new moon."

"Why?" I asked. "I mean I know you're first-class crazy, but why go to all this trouble?"

"Well, I could say, *because I can*." He glowered at me. "But since you pose no threat to me, a small hint wouldn't hurt. I need to have his memory. Unfortunately, that means draining his essence to get what I need."

Primus didn't sound or look anything like I had expected. Everyone thinks of bad guys as big and scary. They have deep voices and raspy laughs. This guy sounded like a used car salesman or a radio announcer. His voice was deeper than Lisa's, but it was as soft and pleasant as a sunny spring day. Then there was the matter of him being really short, and let's not forget his bald head.

Primus sighed. "The adults are gone. Everyone left town, except for old Mootpah, but I was sure he planned a surprise for me. That would be you. Did he give you an orange crystal? Look around, do you see any shadows?"

"You know, Dusty's going to kick your carcass around this cave like an old soccer ball." I said, flicking my tail.

Primus let out a high-pitched, nasally giggle. "It was you that convinced me that I was making this way harder than necessary. There was no need for me to prolong this form by feeding on guardians and their little heroes. Yes, it's fun to torment everyone. But with billions of humans to feed from, life just became a buffet." He giggled again.

"I just need to wipe everybody out all at the same time in the most terryifing way possible. Now that I have the moon horse, I don't need you, Liosa, or Grimalkin." Primus swaggered along the cave wall.

"Dusty will be sufficient for the task."

"You know your giggle is pathetic, right? It's so prissy. Oh, and that task, what kind of task?"

He wagged a short, stubby finger at me. "No spoilers."

Dusty's side and shoulder bore cuts and scrapes. I could see he was hurting. Down deep in my tail, it was his fading little by little that worried me. Pink crystals were fastened to him. I went to bat them off, but Primus stopped me.

"I wouldn't take those off," he said. "They're the only things keeping him alive. I need the horse to fade by tomorrow night, no sooner or later. Just thank me for sparing your life and leave. Oh, and take the camel with you, he smells really bad."

Mark groaned.

A quick look showed thick bands of black fastened around the camel's feet. They reminded me of the same substance Primus's shadow, Magus, was made from. Since blasting Magus was the key to blasting Primus, this was going to be hard. At least the weasel gun should make short work of Mark's bindings, and probably the ones holding Dusty down. The only problem was that I didn't think Dusty could get up. I also noticed Daisy was nowhere to be seen. Hey, I'm observant that way.

I flicked a question with my tail toward the big guy. He commented back "safe" with his ears.

Primus paced. "I don't even know why I bothered sending wentzels after you."

The big guy's breathing grew labored, and the chains holding him down weren't doing him any favors either. He opened his big brown eye and winked at me as he grinned. He seemed very brave. Of course, he was incredibly stupid, too, for agreeing to this nonsense and making me worry. My mind flashed back to poor Jangles.

Now, Dusty wasn't just in Magus's clutches—and we knew from Jangles what that was like, he was in Primus's control, the source of Magus.

"Okay, cat. What do you say, how about my deal? Walk away, and I never bother you again. I'll even let the camel go and change him back."

He didn't say anything about Kenzie. The jerk tottered again, wobbling. Every other step he made required him to reach out and steady himself with his hand.

Dusty's ear wiggled out a message to me. "The light bothers him, too. Stall. Did Kenzie bring her flashlight?"

"Don't be bossy. Mootpah gave me something to help. It's just going take a while to bring him down. We have to blast Magus to get Monkey Boy." I flashed a question with my tail.

Dusty winked back at me. He had a plan. Of all the stupid—I should let him die. It would serve him right. Grass Bag had a plan. Why did everyone think it was a good idea to make a plan without letting me and Kenzie in on the details? But I could deal with it, for now.

"Hey Monkey Boy, how about I kick your butt?" Kenzie called. "Oh look, it's the comic relief." Primus laughed.

The light in this cavern wasn't purple like in the bigfoot town. It wasn't orange like sunlight either. Primus used pink light. This light nonsense was beyond me, and I was clueless as to how it all worked, but somehow, I doubted we would see Magus. Just then Dusty flicked me a message with his ears.

"Did you bring anything to make shadows?" he asked. "Yes, but I don't know how long we could make Primus's shadow appear," I said back. "We were warned that he could probably take a lot of hits."

"You don't have to make his shadow appear, Lisa saw this coming. Make my shadow."

I remember Fuzzy's words about shadow magic, "...and some heroes." We didn't need to make Magus appear, we just needed shades of our own.

"Kenzie," I called. "Change of plan. How about making Dusty's shadow? Remember the bag of light." I turned toward Primus, "Oh, and Monkey Boy, I did warn you Dusty was going to kick you around like a soccer ball."

Kenzie didn't argue. Amazing. A large beam of sunlight hit both me and Dusty at once. Our shadows loomed large across the far cavern wall. Dusty groaned, and his shadow came alive.

"Kenzie, if Monkey Boy lets Maggot out, you know what to do." I yowled.

Dusty's shadow cut loose across the cavern wall. The big guy's shadow was darker than night. It didn't matter that there was pink light, or no light. His shadow glowed dark amber as it raced toward Primus. Maybe there was something to that "moon horse" business.

His shade closed in on Primus in seconds. The shadow horse's shoulder rammed into the creep. The pint-sized villain flew hard against the wall and bounced off to the side, but Primus knew how to take a hit.

The little jerk pulled something from a coat pocket and tossed it into the air. It was a glowing yellow orb. The yellow light diminished the pink light and Dusty could breathe easier. Within a blink of an eye Magus appeared. His dark form swelled, nearly swallowing all the yellow light in the cavern.

The shadowed arm of Magus scraped his own sides and just like the night he killed Jangles, he shed weasels like a cat losing its winter coat.

"On 'em,'" Kenzie called out. Beams of orange light pierced the weasels as quick as they poured off Magus, but that meant Magus was free and unhindered. Each time Kenzie hit Magus or a weasel, Primus would feel the blow. The evil shadow made its way toward me and Dusty.

"Kenzie!" I called.

"Little busy," she answered.

It was true. She was knocking down the weasels as quick as they fell, but the bag of light lay on the ground still pointed in my direction. The words of Fuzzy came back to me, racing through my mind. *Some heroes can make shadows too.*

Then I noticed Dusty's shadow going to town on Primus and I had an idea.

"If he can, I can. Just believe, Kitten," I told myself out loud. "You can do this. Everyone needs your help."

Magus raised a shadowed hand and brushed me aside as if I were a bit of dust, but I bounced back into the light in seconds. My shadow sprang to life. It was as if my shadow became a little window in a wall of light. I could see, but so could my shadow. Whatever my shadow saw, appeared in my head. If I wanted my shadow to look at something I saw with my eyes, its head turned to look as well.

Magus was poised to strike Dusty, but my shadow was on him in a second. It had been so long since I hunted, and it felt good to let my inner Kitten loose. My shadow increased in size the madder I got. It was three times the size of Magus as I thought about poor Jangles. My shade's claws shredded at Magus like the upholstery on Mark's couch.

"You're just a fraud, Maggot." Dusty's voice was more of a groan. "Hey Primus, what did Kitten call you again? Monkey Boy? You really do look better in pictures than in real life."

"That's a good one," I agreed.

This shadow stuff was actually pretty easy, until one of the weasels came at Dusty and me. Kenzie brushed my shade lightly with the weasel gun and sent my body flying across the cavern.

"Hey," I screamed. "Watch what you're shooting at!"

"Sorry," Kenzie said.

Magus raised up a shadowed arm and struck Dusty hard across the side.

Primus let out a cackle.

Dusty's shadow flickered and then disappeared.

I wobbled to my feet. "Dusty, tell your shadow to get up and get moving."

Kenzie pointed her weasel gun and hit the shadow chains on Mark, then on Dusty.

I was back in the light and my shadow had returned. It

was larger than Magus. Unsurprising, really, when one considers the magnitude of my personality. Primus was a runt, and yet he could produce a big nasty shade like Maggot. My shadow smacked and raked at Magus.

"That's for Jangles," I cried.

Dusty's shadow sprang from the floor and bounded toward Primus's shade. The little creep, Primus, was again sent flying as the shades made contact. Primus was back up in a flash.

"Concentrate on Magus," Dusty cried.

In that moment, the big guy and I tag-teamed old Maggot. I would swipe and rake him with shadow claws while Dusty's shadow would wheel and plant two back feet square into the darkest part of Magus's form.

The weasels had stopped coming out of Magus, so Kenzie was taking careful aim to hit him where it counted. A tentacle began to form, but Kenzie hit it with a narrow beam of orange light. We kept at Maggot, again and again until Primus let out a groan and began to wail.

"We have him," Kenzie cried.

"Dusty two, Moron zero." I flicked a nervous glance at Kenzie.

"Weasel burgers!" Kenzie poured on the gunfire. Her eyes glowed all cat-like, as if she were a mouser playing with her first kill. I was so proud of her.

Primus raised a hand above his head. A purple orb appeared above him and rose to the top of the cavern. It flashed. For a moment, I couldn't see anything. I really doubt Kenzie or Dusty could either, but when the sparkles before my eyes cleared, all that was left was Fuzzy's bag of light which sputtered and sparked.

"Did you see that, Kitten?" Dusty whispered, still on his back.

"The bald midget is a show-off," I said. "He also got away."

"Doesn't matter," Dusty rasped. He managed a big horsey grin. "The village is safe now. I think it's time for me to go."

"Wait." My shade vanished, and so I sprang toward the big guy. "Go where? Kenzie, he's barely breathing. What do we do?

"I don't know," she said.

Kenzie yanked the medallion from her pocket, the one Lisa left for us at the ranch, and let it fall to the ground.

It glowed molten red.

"It's alright, Kitten," said Dusty's shadow. "We saved the day. Time for me to go. Please help Mark get changed back."

Dusty's shade flickered against the wall and vanished. The big guy expelled a huge breath and the sound of his beating heart fell silent.

CHAPTER 22

Daisy to the Rescue

Kenzie lit up the cavern with all eleven hundred lumens as she ripped apart the weasel gun.

"What do we do, Kitten?" Kenzie asked.

"Dusty, did your plan include Daisy?" I asked. "Is she near?"

Mark groaned and paced the cavern's edges.

"You can't die, Dusty," I said. "Dying couldn't have been part of your plan."

I wanted to smack him, not that he would feel anything. How could he put himself in danger for us without asking? What kind of stupid plan doesn't involve me being here to watch his back? I set to pacing.

"How can we help?" Kenzie asked again. "Kitten, put your paw on the medallion and call for help."

"Why?" I asked. "What will that do?"

"Just do it."

I let out a big yowl as I placed my paw on Lisa's token. Nothing happened.

"Do it again, Kitten."

I yowled.

This time the cavern lit up. Daisy and a frail, old woman appeared in front of us. The woman was thin, and her white skin seemed as if it might tear like paper. With one hand she carried a reusable cloth shopping bag while she clung to Daisy's mane with the other. She limped a little as they moved forward.

"You really cut this close, cat," the old woman said. "All right, Daisy, I'll set the bag down. You get ready." Daisy nuzzled the woman and nickered softly. "Kenzie, be a dear and take the new stone out of the bag. Then place my medallion on top of it."

"Who are you?" Kenzie shook her head and did as she was asked. "Ah, never mind. Just help Dusty."

"Where's Mark?" The old woman looked about. "Come here." The camel shuffled over. His head drooped and there were water stains under his eyes. "Is the medallion on the stone?"

"Yes," Kenzie said. "Who are you again?"

"Good, Kenzie. Step twenty paces back. Mark, you crowd close. Kitten, get in here. I'm sorry, dear, my name is Liosa."

I stepped back instead of getting closer. She didn't look anything like the Lisa I'd met. But the old woman scolded me. "Where do you think you're going? You get back in this huddle right now."

I tucked my tail and moved in.

"All right, Daisy." The woman's voice was as shaky as her legs. "Everyone is here. Do as I instructed you earlier."

Daisy let out a shrill call and the old woman glowed brightly. This new stone was different from the old one. It was twice the size and completely clear.

"Very good, Daisy." She cast her gaze down at Dusty. "Now, lazybones." She prodded Dusty with her foot. "There's no time to waste. Get up. Primus got away, and he isn't going to take his defeat kindly. You have work to do."

Dusty didn't move.

"Get up," the woman said again.

"Oh no," Kenzie wailed. "He's gone."

His chest neither rose nor fell. The big guy lay still on the ground.

"He's just clowning around again." The woman nudged him, harder with her foot. Dusty still didn't move.

The stone lit up and glowed white, then gold, and finally silver, making the cavern as bright as a full moon on clear night. Dusty's chest expanded like a balloon, and all of his cuts and gashes disappeared.

His shadow appeared across the cavern and raced about, leaping through the air. It galloped toward us and took one great leap back inside the big guy. Dusty stirred.

"Alright, everyone," the woman said. "Your time is wasting."

Dusty was on his feet, but he wobbled some, and when he took a step, he limped on his right front. He was breathing hard and sweating. Then he greeted the woman with a big kiss.

"Don't ever think I abandon my own, especially when they have done everything they were supposed to do without a single complaint." She smiled and kissed Dusty again, on the lips.

"Ewww, horse slobber," I said. "Hay breath."

She looked me. "And you..." She pointed a long, thin finger at my nose.

Here it comes.

She was going to tell me what a foul-up I was. That I caused more problems than I solved. She would scold, and then probably throw something at me. There was no way

I was even going to look her in the eyes.

"You were perfect." The old woman nearly chirped. "I'm sorry we couldn't tell you everything, but we needed you to be...you. You were the distraction needed to beat...what did you call him?"

"Monkey Boy!" Kenzie replied.

She laughed, long and hard. "We Guardians have an uncanny ability to see things coming long before they actually show up." She scooped me up in her right arm and spread her left into the air. Dusty and Daisy closed in to me and her to form one big group hug. "Kitten, you provided just enough chaos to do something that hasn't happened to Primus in a thousand years: keep him guessing."

"Don't forget Kenzie," Dusty said.

The old woman snickered and beckoned to Kenzie. "When your life span is as long as ours, it's hard to surprise any of us. In my younger days, I would have been a match for Primus and his shade, Magus. Even with the moon in its current stage. But not anymore. My days of going toe-to-toe with him are nearly over. We need to go."

CHAPTER 23

The Way Home

We returned to the Bigfoot Village. The streets glowed with crystals that radiated a soft blue light, making it easy to see where we were going. The feldspar no longer glittered with daylight, so the sun must have set. A whole day completely gone. Time flies when you're fighting for your life and humanity.

Everyone shuffled along. Kenzie could barely keep her eyes open.

I yawned. "Lisa, you said you couldn't face off directly against Monkey Boy, does that include Moron too?"

"Moron? Is that what Grimalkin is calling Primus's shade?

"No, I thought that up. And Dusty renamed it Maggot." "You also said Monkey Boy, is that from the word Primate?" Lisa laughed. "Yes, it has been a long time since I could best him, but, you and Dusty didn't seem to have any problems with old Monkey Boy."

Her laugh sent joyful quivers up my tail. For a brief second I felt as if I were lying in the cool dirt on a hot August afternoon. Then she let out a loud, deep belly laugh.

The old woman's hard laughter lit up the dark city

with a silver hue. Daisy thought she might fall over so the dark horse came along her side. Lisa steadied herself against the big guy and Daisy.

"It was important for me to keep my distance from you all this time. I'm very weak right now. Besides, Dusty did all the hard work, with the help of Kitten and Kenzie. You all humiliated Moron the Maggot, and severely weakened Monkey Boy. There is still a lot at stake."

Dusty nodded. "He won't forget this. I'm sure he'll be back. May we go home now?"

Lisa's face went from a smile to a frown as her shoulders slumped a little.

"What do you mean by *a lot at stake*?" Kenzie asked.

Lisa kept us moving even though I really wanted to lie down. I couldn't stop yawning. Still, I wanted answers too. Of course, Lisa also didn't answer Kenzie's question.

"Kenzie should have been with her cousin all this time." I said. "There's also the matter of changing Mark back. What are we going to tell him when he's human again?"

"Well, I'm going to bend a few rules," Lisa said, still without answering Kenzie's question. "Just this once."

Dusty sneezed.

"Okay, I've done it a total of five times and this will make six." Lisa reached out to put her arm around Kenzie and pulled her close, kissing her cheek. "Bending rules is a lot of fun. Who knows? I could be forming a bad habit, but there are good reasons for our rules. If we break this particular rule without careful thought the Mississippi might flood again, or there could be an avalanche in the Andes, maybe the west coast might fall into the ocean. Sure, everyone thinks about all the people who died in the Great Blizzard of 1888 when one of us broke the rule, but there were so many more we saved. No one ever remembers the positive things."

I brushed against Lisa's cheek and purred. "Kenzie is worth it."

The girl gazed over at me and grinned.

"Kenzie," Lisa said. "Kiss Dusty, Daisy, Kitten, and Mark good-bye. You have a cousin who is anxious to see you. Also, Mark needs his phone and truck keys."

"Wait. I don't want to leave now."

Lisa gave the girl a long, slow wink.

Kenzie didn't say another word and handed her the

keys, phone, new moonstone, and everything else.

"How am I going to get there? Will Mark pick me up on his way back? What am I going to say?"

Lisa smiled. "Nothing, because I'm not only going to send you *where* you need to be, but *when* you needed to be there."

"I don't have my things and—"

"Not to worry. Grimalkin has taken care of everything. Now give me a hug and go have fun."

Kenzie gritted her teeth but did as she was told. I was pretty sure she really wanted to stay, but somehow, she couldn't resist. She handed Lisa the medallion.

"Would you like to keep that?" Lisa asked.

"Does it have magic?" Kenzie asked.

"That depends. It might." Lisa smiled.

Lisa set me down on the ground. Then Kenzie planted one last smooch on the old woman's cheek. The girl then evaporated from sight.

"She's a small girl and hardly a strain on my abilities. If I did everything right, she won't remember any of this, and there will be a plane ticket home for her in Fort Smith."

"And if you did it wrong?" Dusty asked.

"She might show up in Hawaii, or standing with the dinosaurs in the cretaceous period. Not to worry, I'm very sure she's fine."

"What about Mark?" Dusty snorted. "How do we get him back?"

"The real problem is he's wearing something he shouldn't be. Did any of you notice the strange blue halter he has on? It won't fit a horse, so why would it be at Mark's place?"

"It came in a box," I said.

"If you take it off," the woman said. "I bet Mark will be his old self, minus a few memories. Actually, I'm going to give him some new memories to replace the old ones. It won't be perfect, and he may have some problems later on."

I traded glances with Dusty and Daisy. "It can't be that simple."

Lisa nodded, but said, "You're not going to do that right now. It would be best to wait until you get home."

"Even at home we're not going to do it," I added. "None of us have thumbs or hands."

"Wait, this isn't over," Dusty said. "Monkey Boy got away. We stopped him for now, but how are we going to deal with him in the long term?"

Monkey Boy? Dusty was finally learning. It made me tingle all the way to the tip of my tail that I finally schooled him in this.

Lisa wrapped her arms around Dusty's neck and hugged him. "You are my brave horse." Then she turned and embraced

Daisy. "I love you both so much. Trust me on this."

"*Meworr*," I said.

She scooped me up in her arms and held me close.

"Tomorrow is the new moon. You have to plant this stone on the property of your home, when you are all together, and no later than lunar noon of that day. Anyone that is not there will not have the protection of the stone bound to them."

"Red," I said. "Do we have to include rubber-lips?" Dusty raised an eyebrow at me and gave me a look.

"Maggot is waiting for us, isn't he?" Daisy's voice was high and sweet.

Dusty's eyes went wide, and his ears perked up. "When

did you..."

A dainty smile tugged at Daisy's mouth. "I think it happened with the new stone and the seed."

Lisa's face lit up, her mouth opened, and her eyes brightened. "How delightful!"

"Wow! Did you know this would happen?" I asked.

"No," she said, putting me down. "I do love pleasant surprises, and after all these eons, surprises are hard to come by. Now, hurry home. You must bond the stone together at your new home as quickly as possible. Daisy will know how to do it when the time comes. This one is new and improved."

Mark's truck drove into the village square where the murals were.

"How'd they get that through that entrance?" I asked. "Better yet, how are we going to get it out of the entrance?"

"Magic," Lisa said.

Little Fuzzy popped out of the driver's seat. Instead of greeting Lisa or Daisy, he reached down and stroked my head. I arched my back in response. Bigfoots have remarkable taste.

"I worry bout you, Kitten," Fuzzy said.

The truck tire had been fixed, and someone had cleaned away all the mud and dust from the outside. It was marvelous to view my fine feline attributes in the reflection on the door, courtesy of the clean surface, and Lisa's glow. I batted my eyelashes at myself. "You beautiful hunk of cat."

"Fuzzy will take you all back," Lisa said. "Maggot—oh, I like that name—will probably have something nasty in store, but one crisis at a time. Fuzzy will remove the halter when you're ready."

"Couldn't we take it off now?" Dusty asked.

Lisa stroked Mark's neck. "Let me ask you this...Why does Mark want to take pictures of the forest people?"

"I don't know. He's always taking my picture," Dusty answered.

"Dusty poses all the time." Daisy rolled her eyes. "Everyone who comes up to him takes his picture. It's annoying."

The big guy straightened and flashed his profile for everyone to see. "Mark says I have a Facebook page and ten thousand followers. Whatever that is."

Lisa sighed. "The forest people and Mootpah wish to recognize the great service you've provided them. But they humbly beg that you keep any knowledge of them and their dwellings secret."

"Mark needs his pictures. It's how he pays for our hay." Dusty tossed his mane. "It's important to him."

Daisy changed the subject. "Are you sure Fuzzy can do this?"

"He has thumbs," I said. "It can be tough to hang on to the steering wheel without them." I held up a front paw and stuck out my claws. "These are almost as good. After watching Kenzie drive, I think I could get us home."

"Thank you, Kitten." Lisa bent down and stroked my head. "I don't think you can work the pedals and steer at the same time. You're not tall enough."

"I take you through a moon tunnel." Fuzzy reached into his fur and pulled out a bright red shirt with large flowers all over it, and a wide-brimmed straw hat.

"Do you have pockets in that hair, or do you keep stuff in...other places?" I asked.

Dusty gave the Bigfoot a doubtful glance. "Kenzie said something about a permit and license to drive. We don't want to break laws."

"I drive through tunnel only. It be all right." Fuzzy opened the back gate of the trailer. "We clean all gear and load it. Even saddle."

"Well, I don't know." Daisy nudged Lisa with her nose. "Does Fuzzy really know how to drive?"

"Oh, yes," Fuzzy interrupted. "I read manual and we get cable television in Mootpah's office. I learn from episodes of Starsky and Hutch."

"There. See? It'll be fine, dear." Lisa patted Daisy's neck. "I've told him what to do."

"He's only a little kid," I said. "Are you sure?"

Fuzzy thrust out his chest. "I seventy-five and a half."

Dusty headed for the back of the trailer.

"Yes, I know that seems very young." Lisa patted Fuzzy's shoulder. "He's mature for his age and will do just fine, I promise."

"I got shotgun!" I cried.

CHAPTER 24

The Ride Home

The ride home wasn't as fun as the ride to the mountains. Mark would have said Fuzzy drove like an old farmer with a new pickup. I was already missing Kenzie.

"Can't we go any faster?" I asked.

"We do speed limit," Fuzzy said.

I peeked out the window at the glittering walls of the moon tunnel. "I really doubt there's a speed limit in here."

The silvery sides glistened with streaks of gray and black.

Fuzzy reached in his fur and pulled out a Ziploc bag.

"Do you have pockets in there or something?" I asked.

Carefully, he held the bag in both hands and still kept the wheel in place with his knee. He grinned. "Cruise Control."

His long fingers made short work of opening the bag and an intoxicating odor filled the cab. He made me wish I had thumbs too.

"That doesn't smell like tuna," I said. "It smells better."

"Salmon." Fuzzy handed me the open bag and grabbed the wheel. "We fish and catch from rivers all over world. You try."

"You fish all over the world?" I gobbled down a strip.

"*Hmmmm.* How do you get there?"

"Shadow portals. Mootpah teach me. We also good at hiding with light."

I sniffed the salmon and gave it a little lick. My legs lost all their strength as I fell upon the bag. This was delightful.

By my fourth mouthful, my tail stood straight up with the tip forming a little question. "This is so good!"

"Fuzzy feel bad I not tell you everything about plan."

"This almost makes up for it." I squinted at him. "Almost."

He reached in his fur again, pulled out another bag, and grinned. "How 'bout now?"

I purred. "We're good."

The truck lurched, bounced, and dropped down with a sudden jerk. It sent me sprawling against the inside of the windshield. Fuzzy trilled and then let out a growl. When he finally leveled us out, the truck and trailer dropped like a stone from a bridge.

Fuzzy was buckled in his seat. Me? I bounced around the truck cab like a rubber ball, fluffed-out tail and everything.

"Weasel action!" I shouted.

He pulled out the little bag of light he had retrieved from Kenzie, took the draw strings in his teeth and pulled. The bag ripped open and a burst of yellow sunlight broke into the cab and out through the windshield. He held the wheel steady with one hand, pulled a small black circle from behind his ear and flung it into the sunlight. It passed through the windshield and grew into an enormous black portal. The last thing I remembered from the truck was being plastered against the back wall of the cab as the truck and trailer shot through a black hole.

We set down flat as if the truck and trailer landed on a cushion. All things considered, this went a lot smoother than Kenzie's near crash at the beginning of our journey. Me? I bounced hard off the windshield and into the truck's seat. My tail was completely puffed out.

"You wear seatbelt next time," Fuzzy scolded.

"I'm a cat, and there are no cat-sized seatbelts. Besides, I don't get to ride in the truck very often."

Fuzzy turned the little key thing, but the truck didn't start.

Bang. Bang. Bang. Dusty wanted out.

Memories of Primus threatening us in the cave came flooding through my head.

"What's going on?" Daisy called out.

"Let us out, Fuzzy." The big guy was hollering now. "Something's wrong. We're in danger."

Fuzzy saw my tail and hustled to get everyone out, but by then, my tail had calmed down.

It was night and we had landed in a place not all that different from the ranch. This night sky held two moons, one great silver circle and the other a blazing red crescent. Cold, white stuff covered the ground, and it also floated softly from the sky in little flakes. I jumped to the ground and stuck my tongue out to taste the fluff.

"It's snow," Daisy said, joining me. "We have it at the ranch in winter. You've never seen it before, have you?"

"Snow?" I let one of the white flakes land on my paw. "It's kind of cold, and no, it doesn't really snow in Seattle."

Dusty and Mark joined us.

"What happened?" Dusty demanded.

Fuzzy fumbled the bag of sunlight from his fur and dropped it in the snow. The way the night sky turned to morning made me think of the blinds Mark opens and closes in the house.

"We high-jacked," Fuzzy said. "Truck fall, and Kitten's tail say danger. I think quick and make escape to sacred place."

"What's the sacred place?" Daisy asked.

"It's where we were born." Dusty let out a loud call and listened for a response. "Don't you remember?"

Daisy shook her head.

"Follow me," Dusty said.

The big guy headed out at a brisk walk. Fuzzy scooped me up and followed.

Dusty led us through a forest of evergreens and up a hill to a lone pine tree on its top. A gray stone, about Kenzie's height, stood under the tree. The stone had a picture of a six-legged horse carved onto its surface.

"Mama told all of us, my brothers and sisters, about Sleipnir when we were foals. It's the first thing we heard from the moment we could stand." Dusty breathed in the cool air and lifted his nose into the breeze. The wind picked up speed.

"How come I don't remember?" Daisy asked.

"I don't know, but I do," Dusty said.

A short, bald figure appeared from out of nowhere.

"Such a tedious story. Save it for another time."

"Oh look everyone, Moron and Primate are back for another butt-kicking," I said. "Ready to lie down, Monkey Boy?"

He raised his hands. "This is a sacred place. We are not permitted to fight." He scowled. "There are some rules even I can't break, at least not yet."

A big grin appeared on Fuzzy's face. "Too bad Kenzie not here. She not bound by those rules."

I flashed the claws on my right paw.

"You bound by rule, too." Fuzzy squeezed me. "Behave."

"I must compliment you, Bigfoot. Isn't that what humans call your kind now?" Magus slogged through the snow toward us. "I would have brought the truck down in a very different place with extremely fatal results. Again,

I have been surprised."

Dusty grinned. "You're getting old, Monkey Boy."

Primus winced. The name really stung him, but he rolled his eyes and continued. "Since I couldn't get you in Liosa's moon tunnel, and there's nothing I can do here, my best strategy is to trap you until you break Liosa's curfew. Your new stone will do you no good here. "

"Can he do that, Fuzzy?" I looked about for the idiot's shade, Magus. It wasn't around. There was no way I was going to trust anything he had to say.

The Bigfoot shrugged. "Truck not start."

"Mark could get it going," Dusty said. "Fuzzy, can you remove the halter?"

Fuzzy didn't answer.

"Why don't you tell them, Fuzzy?" Primus asked. He widened his eyes in mock empathy and tilted his head to the side. Then he snickered, tilted his bald head back, and roared with laughter.

"What's so funny?" Daisy asked.

"The bridle," Primus said. "It has certain safeguards. The only way it will come off is at the same place it went on, and it must be removed no later than set of the new moon, which will be happening very soon."

"Liar," I huffed. "We could do it here."

"Tell them, Bigfoot. Tell them why they can't."

"Sacred ground neutral. Magic cancels all other magic out. Mark come as camel, must leave as camel."

"Dude, seriously? You have the lamest rules." I flicked my tail. "Did you all just take a stupid pill one morning and then make these things up?"

Primus grinned, a long, wicked, nasty grin. "If you don't do as Liosa said, the horses will be relocated. That's not even the worst of it. I'm going to have a storm flatten your home. Nothing will be standing so the camel and the cat will have a nice, empty piece of ground to live on. Oh, and the formalities must be observed. I invoke the rules of parley."

"Red!" Daisy whispered. "He's in danger."

Then, a pang of sadness made me wince. "The mice, they're in trouble too."

"You cost me a victory, moon horse, you and that mangy cat. I may not have gotten what I wanted in the cave, but by the time I'm done, you'll be begging to trade the secret for your release." Primus faded from view. "If you need me, I'll be enjoying my victory."

CHAPTER 25

Not Home Yet

You can't interfere," Fuzzy said. "Rules."

"I'm not interfering, Boyo," Grimalkin said. "I'm impartially observing."

The gray cat stretched and sauntered toward the pickup. "Allow me to get that door for you, Kitten." He twitched his ears and whiskers. The truck door popped open. "I so love good salmon, and there are no better chefs than the forest people."

I leapt inside the truck to guard Fuzzy's present from Grimalkin. "These were given to me."

"Oh," His ears drooped along with his whiskers. "Far be it from me to intrude on another's meal."

Dusty waggled his ears at me, scolding me for not sharing. After everything that had happened, I deserved my treats, but Dusty pawed at the snow and swished his tail.

Daisy coughed and nodded.

"Grimalkin, would you care for some of my salmon?" I didn't want to share.

"Indeed I would!" The cat was up in the truck and started on my second bag in a flash. He had no need of thumbs to get it open and downed the tasty treat in seconds. "*Ooooh*, that was good." He licked his lips and paws and then set to wiping his face.

"Oh, Grimalkin," Dusty said. "Mama once said the rules of hospitality demanded tit for tat."

"Oh, a quid pro quo," the cat purred. "It does seem appropriate, but what should I offer? I can't grant you anything that would interfere with the rules of parley."

"You could start by explaining what the rules of parley are," Daisy snorted. "Why can't we just go?"

"Well, when my kind squabble, we are none too gentle. When the war between my kind grew worse, it distressed most of creation, so this place was set aside by all and...enhanced. If the rules of parley are invoked by someone that has a disagreement with you, all parties involved are trapped here until the matter is resolved to the satisfaction of all belligerents. No one here leaves until the matter is resolved."

A cold gust blew over us.

"That could take forever," Daisy said. "We could die before that happens."

"This place was designed for my kind after all, and not for your short lives. Liosa was fond of using this place for the raising of her moon horses." The cat sighed. "Unfortunately, it is rather binding for Dusty and you."

"But not me," I said. "Send me back to warn everyone. The mice...I mean, Red is in danger."

"I'm afraid you've attached your fate to Dusty when you came to his aid."

"And Fuzzy?" Daisy asked.

"Well, he and the forest people are bound to this place too."

Grimalkin gazed at us all and flicked his tail.

"Oh, so you've decided to stick your nose into this." A large, black shadow moved over us, blotting out the sun. "I don't recall inviting you."

It was Magus, the shade of Primus.

"Prior claim according to the agreement with Liosa," Grimalkin said from the hood of the truck. "I mustn't be negligent, or it shall come back upon my good name." The cat didn't look up from his grooming.

"Hah! What good name?" Magus scoffed.

"I hear the big fella there has quite the name for you." He gazed at Dusty. "Can you share it with the rest of us, Dusty?"

"Maggot," Dusty said.

"I didn't catch that, Boyo," Grimalkin added. "Can you say it louder?"

Dusty cleared his throat. "Maggot."

Magus drew his inky shadow into a human shape and posed with his arms crossed in defiance. Then something curious happened. The snow brightened like the screen in Mootpah's work area—the shadow screen. Magus's shadow flickered against the ocean of white.

"I got a couple of names for him too," I said. "Would you like to hear mine?"

"That would be a treat, since we have time to kill," Grimalkin said. "What names have you come up with?"

"I know his other name is Primus, so Kenzie suggested *primate* at first." At the mention of the name, Magus winced. "But I changed it to Monkey Boy, and for the both of them at the same time, there's Moron."

Daisy raised her eyebrows. "What's a monkey?"

"Allow me." Grimalkin stood to his feet.

"*Meooooow.*" The gray cat's body grew taller as he stood up on his hind legs. His tail grew longer and thicker, and the cat's face widened and grew rounder. His ears

303

shrank into human-like contraptions. His eyes turned brown and moved close together.

Grimalkin twittered like a little bird and walked around on his back feet, using his tail to balance. Daisy burst out laughing. Grimalkin hopped down off the truck and clambered up Daisy's legs like a tree. He picked at her mane and ears, as if he were searching for ticks and other bugs.

"Monkey Boy, Primus, primate," I said. "Moron."

Grimalkin chittered away and jumped up and down across Daisy's back.

Everyone cracked up, even Fuzzy. We took turns.

I said, "Monkey Boy."

Dusty echoed back, "Maggot."

We laughed even harder, until Dusty and I said Monkey Boy and Maggot together in unison as Grimalkin did a little monkey jig on Daisy's back.

Magus clutched at his throat and then his chest. His shadow arched across the snow and shriveled to a black stain before he vanished.

We didn't stop laughing until Fuzzy cut loose. He bellowed and trilled so loudly that snow fell off the surrounding pines. That quieted everyone.

"What happened to Maggot?" Daisy asked.

"He's off lickin' his wounds," Grimalkin said. "We caught him by surprise and drained off a nice bit of power. We had a good thing going, but it's this place. It sensed his distress and moved him before he could really be hurt."

"The name thing was kind of fun," Daisy said. "He's such a bully, but the name stuff still doesn't make sense to me."

"You don't need to understand how it works. Just remember that it does." Grimalkin jumped off of Daisy and turned back into a cat. "Remember, names can also build people as well as wound. It's always better to build than tear down."

"You had thumbs," I commented. "Can you teach me to do that? Become that monkey-thing"

He blinked at me. "The most important thing to remember when dealing with a bully is to never surrender your confidence. There's no shame in running, ducking, or avoiding them. Bullies exist everywhere and always shall."

"If this place won't allow us to hurt Primus, it also won't allow him to hurt us," Daisy added.

"He not have to," Fuzzy said. "He just keep you from finishing task."

Dusty turned and walked away. "Hey, where you going?" I asked. "Stretching my legs."

CHAPTER 26

Perpilax

The sun was now high in the sky, but the chilly air set frost hanging off my ears and whiskers. It was getting colder and no one knew what to do. Still, you can only fuss and fume for so long before it tires you out, and you get hungry.

Fuzzy broke out horse blankets for Dusty and Daisy. They found a spare blanket for Mark while Grimalkin and I shared a saddle blanket. Then came the barbeque and a portable fire pit.

The Bigfoot thought of everything. He set up a camp chair for himself and settled into it.

"I think this call for a little hospitality," Grimalkin said with a long, slow wink. The cat flicked his tail, and a nice fire appeared. "Dusty, you mentioned a story your Ma told you. Care to share it with the rest of us?"

"It hardly seems like the time," Daisy said. "Besides, I don't remember Mother ever telling me the story of Sleipnir."

Fuzzy nodded and moaned.

"It hardly seems like the time," the big guy agreed.

"A good story can inspire when a body is most discouraged." The gray cat waved his tail, a long, slow movement. "I'm sure it's a good story."

Dusty sighed. "Ma told me there was a monster, a big nasty one that lived a long time ago. No one knew where it came from. Some said it was a giant snake. Others said it was an insect. There were a few that called it a dragon. Whatever the thing was, it was hungry all the time and ate almost anything it came upon." Dusty shifted his feet and moved a little closer to the fire.

"Did the monster have a name?" I asked. "What did it look like?"

"It had a long snake-like body and a big alligator head with rows of long, sharp teeth."

Grimalkin purred and the gray smoke of the fire swirled into a cloud and then took the shape of Dusty's monster.

"What was its name?" Daisy snorted. "Dragon or..."

"Norbert?" Fuzzy glanced around at our blank faces. What?" he said. "It might have been."

"Mama called him the Perpilax." Dusty yawned.

Grimalkin's green eyes glowed in the firelight as his purring grew softer.

"The Perpilax had bright green scales harder than

concrete and fangs as long as Mark's truck. He was ten times larger than our barn and slithered from place to place like a snake."

Fuzzy fetched buckets from the trailer and filled them out of the water tanks on Mark's truck. When he set them down next to the horses, Dusty took a drink.

"The Perpilax was particularly fond of snacking on towns and the people who lived in them. He considered them tasty, kind of like the way Kitten prefers mice."

The smoke formed buildings and streets, showing the monster gliding toward them.

"Oh, I've given up eating mice," I said. "Salmon is my new favorite, but I still won't turn down tuna if offered."

Dusty's eyes widened in surprise at the mention of the mice. "Well, there were heroes that came to fight him, but they were defeated with ease."

Small stick figures formed in the smoke. They took their place on the illusory streets but were gobbled down by the Perpilax. Other figures formed, but they ran away once the monster consumed the heroes.

"As the story goes, one day a big, quiet guy with an eye-patch arrived."

The smoke drawings whisked away in a breeze and the smoke began to form a new shape.

"What was his name?" Grimalkin asked.

"Mama told me it didn't matter—it was the horse he rode that was important. The horse's name was Sleipnir."

The smoke circled, changed its form, and took on the shape of a horse.

"Why was the horse important and not the rider?" Daisy asked.

"Sleipnir was the real hero. He had six legs and ran faster than the wind. And he could fly." Dusty took another drink of water. "He was as yellow as a full moon on a summer's night, but the most interesting thing was that he could talk."

The smoke horse grew two extra legs and reared up.

Dusty cast a glance at Grimalkin. The gray cat returned his gaze with a nod.

I hopped off my blanket to get a closer look. Fuzzy eyeballed me and patted his lap. I obliged by joining him. He might be hairy and stinky, but his lap was nice and warm. Besides, the story was getting interesting.

"The rider, we'll call him Patch, charged the monster

straight away," Dusty resumed. "He sliced, cut, and parried with all kinds of blades and pointed weapons. The Perpilax's skin was hard, and the weapons did almost nothing to harm the monster. But Patch didn't give up. He kept the Perpilax busy for days, weeks, months, and years. People weren't being eaten and towns weren't being destroyed, but he was making a mess of the landscape by raising new mountains, flattening old ones, changing the course of rivers and streams. The fight was looking as if it would never end."

"But no one was being eaten, right?" I asked.

"That does little good if your barns are being flattened just after rebuilding," Daisy said.

It seemed the rider and horse would have to keep fighting forever just to save people from harm.

The smoke began to animate itself as the smoke puppets of Patch, Sleipnir, and the Perpilax fought in mock battles.

Grimalkin's eyes narrowed to green slits, and his ears twitched forward and back. He was listening, but not just to Dusty's story. I know, because I heard the faint shuffle of footsteps outside the circle of warmth.

"The unthinkable happened," Dusty said. "On the spring solstice, the height of the Perpilax's strength, the rider was unseated and knocked unconscious. Everyone thought it was over, nothing could stop the monster, and everyone despaired."

"Why?" Fuzzy asked. "Couldn't they run away?"

"I asked Mama the same thing," Dusty said. "She explained that with monsters as big as the Perpilax, there would eventually be nowhere to run. He would consume everything."

"Sounds like a dire situation," Grimalkin said. "What was the outcome?"

"Sleipnir stepped between the monster and his rider, to protect Patch. When the Perpilax tried to consume the rider, Sleipnir withstood him. He would rise up and strike, wheel around and kick. He caught the monster by surprise and learned that its nose, eyes, and lips were tender. No matter how hard the Perpilax snapped and bit, the horse managed to avoid those big jaws, especially since he was fast and could fly."

"Not buying it," Fuzzy said. "Horse too little to do good."

"You never had to deal with biting flies in the pasture," Daisy said. "Small things can be as disruptive as big things. Sometimes worse, when you're so much bigger. Small things are hard to hit."

Dusty continued. "Sleipnir was tiring. He realized that strength alone wasn't going to win the day. He would have to out-think the monster."

"Too true," Grimalkin said. "It was exciting to see."

I blinked. "Wait. You were there?"

"Many of us Gwendolyn were," The gray cat said. "We have always had an interest in this little blue planet."

"Knowing you, the Perpilax was your creation," I said.

"No, the rider was the hero of Primus. The horse was Liosa's."

"I don't understand," Daisy said. "Wasn't Primus..."

"Corrupt?" Grimalkin asked. "Not in those days, but if you ask me, Patch's defeat was the thing that started Primus's downfall. Patch his hero and Primus suffered from a fierce sense of pride. You might call it the fatal flaw of both Patch and Primus."

"Like hero, like patron." I grinned.

"How did that work?" Dusty asked. "Mama never said

anything about that."

"Liosa and Primus had a wager, not that she was interested in such things. It was him that forced it. Liosa has always been loyal to her heroes and would not put up with anything that subjected them to harm. In the end, Primus forced the issue. He bet the horse would get eaten, she bet the Perpilax would be defeated."

"Who won?" I asked.

"Neither." The gray cat yawned.

"How did that happen?" Daisy asked.

"Well, that's just it. None of us know what actually happened, do we, Dusty?"

Dusty picked up the story again. "The rider woke up but decided he couldn't end the life of the beast. So he walked away. Patch called for Sleipnir, but the horse wouldn't come. Sleipnir refused and wouldn't release the Perpilax's gaze, figuring as long as he was looking at Sleipnir, no one could be eaten. You see, Sleipnir and his kin have that commanding gaze, and the ability to communicate on deep levels. Me and Daisy have it too."

"Sounds positively pig-headed to me," I added. "It makes me think of someone else that put himself at risk."

Dusty snorted. "Daisy was right. Bees and flies can be annoying. At first the monster tried to return to munching on people and towns, but Sleipnir buzzed the monster around his eyes and newly-discovered tender spots. Finally, that Perpilax had enough and challenged Sleipnir to a game of riddles. They would ask one another riddles. The first to miss an answer would have to live at the bottom of the ocean and leave the other in peace."

"Sleipnir agreed, but on two conditions: he got to ask the first question, and the first thing out of their mouths was to be taken as the answer—right or wrong," Grimalkin said.

"Hey, I was telling the story." Dusty snorted. "The monster agreed. Sleipnir glowed like the moon when he asked the first question.

Grimalkin's smoke puppets swirled and reset into the Perpilax and Sleipnir. Sleipnir's figure glowed silver.

"He whispered the question into the Perpilax's ear, and..."

"Wait," I interrupted. "Don't we get to hear the question?"

Dusty shook his head. "No sooner had the words left

the horse's mouth than the monster froze like a statue. At first Sleipnir thought the Perpilax had died, but the monster's heart still kept beating. He just wouldn't move."

"Or be moved," Grimalkin added. "It was nearly a decade before the people would even come within a hundred miles of him. They couldn't move him, bury him, do anything with him."

"Sleipnir didn't win," Dusty said. "He caused a stalemate. Perpilax had to say the answer, but it stumped him. The descendants of Sleipnir are there to this very day, guarding and watching, should the monster answer. Then the next moon horse would have to answer the riddle."

"Wait, is that it?" I said. "No, no, you can't end it like that. What happened?"

The smoke swirled into a close-up of the monster and Slepnir. I blinked at Grimalkin.

"It's a story in progress, Boyo. The monster was stumped. Rather than guess wrong, the Perpilax chose to think about it. I was there, and the rules were specific, but not specific enough. The Perpilax found a loophole. He thought and thought and thought. Enough time passed and the thing got covered with dirt. Trees and grass started growing on top of him. He's thinking to this very day. The game is still in play," Grimalkin said. "And I think you-know-who wants the game to resume."

"It's just a story, right?" I flicked my tail at Dusty. "He didn't answer back."

"Sore loser," Fuzzy said. "Rather than go live in the ocean, he chose not to answer."

"That's the point when dealing with us," Grimalkin added. "You must be precise and specific."

"I would like to know what was asked," Daisy said.

"All moon horses are told the exact riddle on the day we leave this place, and the answer. We must ponder the possibility of it being answered and the game continuing."

"What was the riddle?" I asked.

"I can't tell you," Dusty said. "Mama said someone might figure out the answer. All they had to do was find the Perpilax and tell him what to say."

"Don't feel bad." Daisy rolled her eyes. "I wasn't told the riddle, either."

Dusty shook his head. "There can only be one moon

horse at a time. Right now, according to Mama, it's me."

In the light of the fire, I could just see Daisy stick her tongue out at her brother.

Fuzzy's lap was nice and warm, it made me purr. "A riddle? That's all that stopped the creature? Not much of a story."

"That's how the story goes." Dusty nodded.

I caught a glimpse of Grimalkin's face in the fire light. His eyes were narrow slits.

"Grimalkin?" Fuzzy asked. "Where will you take Dusty and Daisy, if the stone isn't reset on Mark's property?"

"Here." Grimalkin didn't bat an eye. "This is where they were born. They will be cared for and kept in safety. It was Lisa's *Plan B* so that no matter what happened, they would always be safe."

Primus strode into camp as if he owned everything. "I'm here to parley, kindly withhold the name calling. I will trade you your freedom for the knowledge of the riddle. I will also promise to no longer pursue you or yours. As you know, I keep my promises to the letter."

"Sounds like a no-brainer to me," I said.

"I can't tell you," Dusty said. "I already promised

Mama."

"I think you will." Primus's shade, Magus, now joined the conversation. Big, ugly blob of black taking up a position behind the bald, short guy.

"No," Dusty said.

"Why?" Magus asked.

Grimalkin interrupted. "You would only use the riddle to wake the monster, provided you could find him and twist his will to your advantage. The moon horse has brains and character."

"Monkey Boy," I cried.

"Maggot," Dusty answered back.

Then we spoke in unison. "Monkey Boy, Maggot."

In a blinding flash the scenery faded before us. An icy wave of cold passed through me and I felt pressure all over as if someone set a bale of hay on top of me.

When the pressure released we found ourselves, our fire, the truck and trailer, and Grimalkin on a cold clifftop overlooking an icy lake.

CHAPTER 27

A Plan?

Now, lads," Grimalkin said. "Let's be a little more judicious in the use of the name calling. We can't get Magus to set you free if he isn't around to do it."

No one was freaking out. I mean, we were sitting in one place, and quicker than a blink, we're somewhere else. That would freak out anybody, but we all hardly seemed to care.

"I'd like to stomp his brains out," Daisy said. "I heard what the kids in Fuzzy's village said about the terrible things he did."

Fuzzy stood up. "Gray cat not supposed to help. You not called to parley. You leave. Rules must be followed."

"Aye, that's true. But technically, I'm not helping, just trying to get you all to let up on Magus. Besides, Kitten offered me hospitality and I still have a quid pro quo to offer back."

The sun was still high in the sky and it was cold, but with all the snow, I had to admit it was pretty.

"I wish Kenzie were here," I said. "She could tell me why it was summer at home but winter here."

Grimalkin winked at me and smiled.

"We need to figure out how to get Primus to let us go,"

Daisy said. "I don't know what time it is or what day, but we must be closing in on our deadline. I don't want to lose my home. I like living with Mark and Dusty on our ranch."

"I could give him what he wants." Dusty pawed the ground. "It's only a story, right?"

"Who cares what he wants?" I said. "It's because he wants it, and as a matter of principle, he ain't getting what he wants."

The big guy's lips were all pouty and his ears lay flat.

"You aren't feeling guilty about Jangles, are you?" I asked. "

"A little. I don't want any of you hurt." Dusty winced, took a deep breath and trotted off.

"Daisy," I said, "you'd best stick with your brother. We don't want Magus talking him into doing something stupid."

Daisy lit out after Dusty.

"Can't you get Lisa to help us out?" I asked Grimalkin.

"If I could interfere, and I'm not saying I would, the answer would be no. In her present state, she's too frail." The old scoundrel stood up and stretched. "Fuzzy, you have any more of that salmon?"

Fuzzy shook his head, but I hadn't eaten all of my portion. "Hey, Grimalkin. Can Magus or Primus hear everything that's being said?"

"In this place, mostly," Grimalkin yawned.

"So if Maggot learns the riddle, what good does it do him?"

"Oh, Boyo, old Magus is in love with chaos. He won't be happy until he unleashes it all and does away with order and everything we love. Unleashing the Perpilax would give him a never-ending source of misery to feed on. He'll figure out the answer, find the Perpilax, and set the monster free. With the Perpilax loose, well, the chaos will be endless."

"It's not that easy," I added. "The Perpilax answers a question, he has to ask one back in order to win. Couldn't we just do the parley thing and hold Magus here?"

"Only one parley at a time. That's the rule."

"I have a little salmon left. Would you like to have it?" I asked.

"Of course. And would you be wanting a second quid pro quo in return?"

I flicked my tail.

CHAPTER 28

Just Desserts

Dusty and Daisy returned at a slow walk. The big guy scowled. His ears were flat back against his skull. Daisy hardly refused to meet her brother's gaze, let alone stand less than five horse lengths next to him. Looked to me like a family squabble.

"What have you two been doing?" I asked.

Dusty shook his head, making his ears flop. "Visiting old neighbors and places we used to go when we were foals."

"And Mama's grave," Daisy said. Her countenance went somber, and her head drooped.

I was sorry I asked and had a sinking feeling I wasn't going to like what was about to happen. It was just like that certain something that fills the air when you're about to get your tail stepped on, and you realize there's nothing you can do to stop it.

"We were talking things over." Daisy snorted.

"She talked. I didn't get a word in edgewise." Dusty pawed the ground and wagged his head at her. "I think I liked it better when she didn't talk so well."

Daisy was ready to bite her brother when Grimalkin interrupted. "Now, you two, let's have no fighting."

"Dusty disagrees with me," she huffed. "I don't care. I'm going to give Primus what he wants."

The big guy flashed a hurt look at his sister. She refused to return the eye contact.

"You decided to tell Maggot the riddle?" I asked. "That's the dumbest thing I've ever heard."

Dusty grinned at me and then nodded. "See?"

"We can't leave Mark like this. Sure, we can live here again, but neither of you will be able to. What about Red?" Daisy added.

"Hey Grimalkin." I jumped up on the truck. "Are you going to let her get away with this? Can't we vote or..."

The gray cat blinked at me and shrugged. "Don't drag me into this. These are your decisions. I'm not allowed to help."

"But you said—" I flicked my tail. Daisy set her jaw and glared at me, daring an argument.

I didn't want Mark to stay a camel, or Dusty and Daisy to lose their home...our home. But giving Monkey Boy what he wanted? That was just wrong.

"Please, Daisy, don't do this," Dusty begged.

"You were the one who said it was just a story." Daisy

wheeled around. "Magus, Primus, whatever you call yourself. I'm going to give you what you want."

The big guy grimaced and flattened his ears, but Daisy ignored him.

Grimalkin yawned. "Well I guess you won't be needing me, but before I go, allow me to do the honors. Primus!" the cat yowled. "Front and center. Show your runty self, and we won't need your Magus either."

The sun's position in the sky had changed, the day was moving forward. A cold, harsh wind blew over us hard enough to make the truck and trailer rock from side to side. The old runt appeared.

Grimalkin faced me and gave me a long, slow wink. "I'll be watching in the background. Honor your choices." He vanished.

"Well?" Primus's voice was soft and shaky. It was hard to believe this short, bald thing—like a used car salesman when he spoke—caused so much trouble.

"This is the riddle as it was relayed to me," Daisy said. "My brother doesn't agree with this decision, so you will hear it from me instead of him."

"Unacceptable," Primus said.

"Too bad," she said. "You, of all people, should understand what breaking one's word does. Since I made no such promise, like my brother, I am under no obligation to keep the secret."

Primus's wrinkled face scrunched into a sneer. "So Dusty loses nothing in this transaction. Yet you don't even remember the story. How can I trust you?"

Daisy batted her eyelashes. "I got my brother to tell me. Do you want the riddle and answer or not?"

His sneer stretched into a mocking grin. Then he laughed. "Of course. Your brother could learn a lot from you. I make the same offer to you. I will let you and yours go in safety, and I will never bother you ever again."

Daisy nodded.

"Please, Daisy, don't do this." Dusty was begging.

"Yeah, I agree. Don't give him what he wants."

Daisy's soft brown eyes were shedding tears. The way she tucked her tail when she moved toward Primus made me realize how hard this might be for her.

She pawed the ground. "In the original story..."

"Wait, I interrupted. "He only promised not to harm you. Not like when he promised Dusty he wouldn't harm

329

you and yours."

"Well? I'm waiting." Daisy tapped her foot.

"Very well, I offer you the same promise and give my word."

"I heard that," Grimalkin's voice said. "Will you be following the traditional stipulations?"

"Mind your own business, cat," Primus muttered.

"Yeah," Daisy agreed. "What Grimalkin said."

The little beast was ready to throw a temper tantrum but relented with a snort.

"Done," Grimalkin spoke.

"You understand that the first thing out of the Perpilax's mouth has to be the correct answer."

"I understand," Primus uttered through gritted teeth. "I was listening even back then, but Sleipnir made it impossible for me, or anyone, to hear. Get on with it."

"One last thing," Dusty added. "When you let us go, you will give us a full day before the new moon."

"Now just one minute," Primus objected. The big, shadowy form of Magus appeared behind him. "I don't have the power."

"Lisa, in her weakest state, just before the new moon,

sent our friend back in time. Are you saying you can't?" Dusty snorted. "What a loser."

Magus puffed up big and black, his red eye glowed bright.

Primus moved toward to Dusty, clenching his fists. "Yes, I agree. Get on with it."

Daisy cleared her throat. "Here is the riddle. You stand in a cave. There are two doorways out of it. One door is the exit, but the other door leads to certain death. Each door has an unconquerable guard. One guard always tells the truth, and the other one always lies. You don't know which guard is which. You are allowed to ask one question to determine which door is the exit out. What question should you ask?"

Primus threw his hands up. "Are you kidding me?" Daisy snorted. "Yes, that's the question."

"You're really not serious."

Daisy nodded.

"Get on with it," Dusty said.

Primus drew back, his eyes wide and his mouth open. "That's so easy. I don't even need you to tell me the answer. You're free to go."

The sky grew gray and overcast in the twitch of a whisker. There, next to Primus, stood a frail old woman. I recognized her this time. She bent over, gripping a walking stick in her hand. Grimalkin rubbed against her leg with a big kitty grin plastered across his face.

"I invoke parley with Primus and Magus," Lisa said. "I, Liosa, so do demand."

The old runt screamed, "You can't do that! I have things to do!"

"I can too, you old scoundrel." She spoke to Fuzzy. "Would you be so kind as to leave one of Mark's camp chairs for me, and a blanket?"

Moron raised his arms and rotated his hands as if he were trying to call up some sort of twister or storm, but the minute the sound of thunder boomed, he was whisked away out of sight. The place had intervened against the threat of harm, this time moving Primus.

Fuzzy complied in seconds, vacating a red chair and leaving the camel blanket.

The woman hobbled over to us, "I told you I don't abandon those who are mine." She spread her arms and gave us each a hug.

Dusty raised his head and flashed that hero profile like he was posing for Facebook. "It worked just as you said it would."

"Now wait just a minute," I said. "Did you...?"

"Quid pro quo number one," Grimalkin said. "You're welcome. Now be off with you."

"Yes," Lisa said. "Before Moron gets over his temper tantrum. He let you go and is not free to do any harm to you in this place or otherwise. Be warned, that doesn't mean other things can't on his behalf, and without his permission."

"He promised," Dusty said.

"He only promised he wouldn't harm Daisy or all of you, but that was after he harmed your home. Grimalkin, where are you?" Lisa clapped her hands.

The gray cat answered with a pleasant little chirp from down at her feet.

"I release Mark from his condition, this one time, for an extra day. Relocation will be allowed and the token reset in a new place, if necessary. I'm very sorry for your loss."

The ground shook and cold wind rushed around us.

The woman seemed genuinely sad. I believed her.

Dusty went quiet. His ears flattened, and he pushed his head into Lisa. "I don't like this arrangement. What about you?"

"Don't worry about me. I can't be harmed in this place. I now have a way of keeping Moron here for as long as I continue on. Now be off with you."

Dusty pouted. I would have thought this to be good news and he would be pushing get to get home. Then again, Lisa did say our home was damaged.

"Grimalkin?" Lisa looked down.

Grimalkin disappeared and then reappeared, hovering in the air, looking Lisa in the eyes. Then his body coalesced as it lowered to the ground. She giggled.

"Could you see them settled?" Lisa asked.

"Of course." The gray cat purred.

Lisa stretched down a wrinkled hand and stroked the old cat. "You are a dear friend. Thank you. You may tell them when they return."

Fuzzy loaded everything in such a blur we hardly had time to breathe.

"I don't want to leave you here." Dusty stuck his lower

lip out. He was cute when he pouted. Small wonder he didn't get his way more often with that routine.

"You must go back." Lisa patted his cheek. "There's more for you to do. More who will need help from you and Kitten."

Daisy lowered her nose and gave me a nudge. It practically sent me flying into the truck. When I recovered my balance, she winked.

There were more goodbyes and ear scratches, followed by tears and sad smiles. The horses helped nudge Mark into the trailer before following him in. Fuzzy, Grimalkin and I climbed into the truck's cab.

The moon tunnel appeared in front of us. From far away, Magus screamed. "You haven't seen the last of me. I have many more allies than you do friends."

Fuzzy put the truck in gear and pushed the accelerator, sending us forward.

"It's true," Grimalkin said as he perched between me and Fuzzy. "He has a lot of help."

"Maybe we just have to make more friends," I answered. "I guess we'll have to do it fast since he seemed to know the answer to the riddle."

"You have more time than you think," Fuzzy said.

"I'm confused. What just happened? Is Primus going to end the world or not?" I looked out the window at the shining walls of the tunnel.

Fuzzy opened his mouth to explain, but Grimalkin stopped him. "Allow me, Boyo." He lowered his body onto the seat to recline. "The one thing Primus, Magus, or Moron has in abundance is pride. There are at least two answers to that riddle, maybe another. Only Sleipnir knew which one he had in mind when he asked the Perpilax. I'm sure the old worm knew this but couldn't decide which one Sleipnir would want. Of course, if Sleipnir ever breathed a word about that answer, he has taken it to his grave. Since Monkey Boy is stuck here indefinitely by parley, we should be fine for the time being, if Lisa can manage to keep herself entertained."

"That doesn't help us if the Perpilax gets loose again. That's a big *IF*," I said.

"Yes and no. Liosa outmaneuvered Primus and found a way to trap him, without having to muscle him. Dusty and Daisy put on a very convincing performance, and so did you."

"I wasn't performing," I said. "Exactly." Grimalkin laughed.

Having Lisa trapped with Monkey Boy made me feel bad. I doubted we would ever see her again. I fished out the Ziploc bag from beneath my seat, and there were just a few mouthfuls of salmon left. I handed it to Grimalkin.

"For me?" The gray cat grinned, and his tail flicked.

"Yes," I said.

"Let me warn you, lad," he said, his expression turning grave. "Moron had your old home flattened by a tornado when you first entered the sacred place. Since there was no stone to protect it, and his promise was not in play, he was free to do so."

"What about Red?" I asked. The red horse was annoying with his rubber lips, but it wouldn't be the same without him.

"He's fine, and so is your little army of mice." Grimalkin devoured the rest of my salmon. "I was watching out for you. Quid Pro Quo number two. I'd say this salmon makes us even."

A thought occurred to me. *Houses and crates can be traded for different ones, but family and friends are irreplaceable.*

The truck appeared back by the house. Just like the gray cat said. It should have been a happy moment, but we saw Magus's parting gift. The land was full of debris and piles of rubble and broken trees for as far as we could see. Once everyone was unloaded, I couldn't miss Dusty's and Daisy's big brown eyes watering. Everything was in ruins. No one said anything as we all stared. The Bigfoot tried to put on a happy face, but all he managed was a fierce kind of snarl. It was totally appropriate.

Fuzzy set Mark's phone and keys on the hood of the truck. "We are day ahead of new moon, thanks to Monkey Boy's promise."

"No wonder he seemed so pleased to let us go. Getting him to agree was easier than it should have been," Daisy said.

The Bigfoot looked around at each of us. "Goodbye, friends. Will see you again." He reached up and pulled off Mark's camel halter. The minute it came off, Fuzzy and the halter vanished from sight, except for a filmy shadow that strode off toward the property line.

Mark stood in front of us, eyes wide and mouth open. He pushed back his cowboy hat and turned in a circle. Light sparkled from small drops spotting his cheek. We all crowded closer.

"What happened? Where...uhm." Mark was struggling to speak.

A gray truck and horse trailer rumbled down our road and into the driveway. We made our way through the broken bits of house and barn as we moved across the ground. The visitor stopped in front of where the hay barn used to stand.

A thin, wiry man with a pinched face and high cheekbones slid from the passenger's side. He wore a gray suit and had the sparkliest green eyes. With a smile, he turned and offered me a slow ponderous wink with his right eye. My tail tingled in response.

"My name is Mr. Grims." He held out his hand, and Mark shook it. "Mr. Peterson, I represent an anonymous client. You were away on your job when the storm hit. There was a tornado and it flattened everything. It was in the local paper. Julie, your hired girl, got Red to safety, but she was unable to find your cat."

Mark exhaled and bent down to scoop me up. He held me close, and I let him. "No one could call me?"

"We tried." Mr. Grims cast a glance at me. The corner of his mouth stretched upward. "Even your employer. I am sorry for your loss, but perhaps this can soften it."

He opened a case in his hand and held out some papers. "My client's granddaughter spent some time in hospital and in one of the homes Mark and Dusty visit. The ones where family members and sick children can stay for free. Mark and Dusty visited them and helped to make a painful time much more pleasant. She never forgot it, and when she passed from this plane of existence recently, she bequeathed you a ranch about eight miles from here." He pushed them into Mark's hand. "You will find everything you need to know in those papers. Of course, you will need to show up at the county courthouse. Papers must be signed, but there's no hurry."

A tall fellow stepped from the driver's side of the truck. He had a big, fuzzy beard and long hair that draped out from beneath a cap. His black t-shirt had words on it that I could read. It said, "Weasel Burgers." He snarled at me and then waved.

Dusty lowered his head and nudged me.

The tall guy had a familiar lumber to his gait. Seeing him sent a warm feeling surging from the tip of my tail, all the way to the points of my ears. After unloading Red from the trailer, he handed Mark the lead rope.

"I sort of remember taking pictures." Mark's face was pale and drawn. Then a small flicker of recognition flashed in his eyes as he glanced down at me in his arms. "I must really be tired. I remember working and all the usual things, but no Bigfoot."

Mr. Grims proffered a knowing look, and for a brief flash, I could see him with gray fur on his face and small pointed ears perched on the top of his head. The tall fellow gave me a wave as they drove off.

Everyone crowded close to Mark and me. For all the mess and desolation, we had come home. Our family was together, Magus and Primus defeated and imprisoned.

The glow of the rising sun peeked through the open windows of my favorite place in our new house. Orange light spread across the ground to the sounds of doves cooing . Out in the front yard glowed an enormous amber crystal. The symbols on the stone seemed to move as the sun filtered through it. I'm not really a morning cat, but after a good prowl this was where I wound down before napping.

Everything looked perfect, including the army of tiny men wearing pointy hats that surrounded my window...

Wait. I blinked my eyes hard, but the little army was still there and my tail had not puffed out, but it sure tingled.

The little men stood guard like the lawn ornaments sold at a street vendor's booth near my old home. The lady who sold them called them lawn gnomes. Those were creepy enough then, but I can tell you they're even creepier now that they showed up at the new house, uninvited. I needed to wake Mark.

I jumped on Mark's head and pawed at his stomach, but he didn't move. So I bit his big toe.

Mark's eyes fluttered open, but he wasn't laughing. He followed me out to the four-season porch, but when he laid eyes on the little men, he burst out laughing.

"Oh, that Kenzie! She must be back from Arkansas."

Mark filled my dish and stumbled back to bed.

Joke or not, these things were driving my tail crazy. Not like "there's weasels out to get us" crazy, but more like "there's magic afoot."

"Hey, Kitten," Dusty whinnied at me from the pasture.

It was still summer. Mark had left the windows open and the screens closed. Since this half of the house served as part of the fence, the horses could come right up to the windows. *Hmmm, I live in a fence post.*

"I think we have a new job," Dusty called.

"What would give you that idea?" I twitched in response with my tail.

Mark made a big deal about me wandering off and getting lost. I mean, really, me get lost? Hah! He confined me to the house until further notice. Tail talk allowed us to chat through the window without shouting. Of course, the horses could use their ears and tails too, but no one cared if they hollered their heads off out in the pasture.

"Let's talk," Daisy agreed.

"I'll be waiting in the spare bedroom," I said with a tail swish. She had been learning tail talk from me in the afternoons. You never know when you might be cornered by an insane fairy and have to converse silently while the villain monologues like a bad cartoon episode.

Dusty and Daisy headed toward the window of the spare bedroom. Red was gone—he had moved in with Kenzie. I missed him, but not his rubber lips.

I bounded onto the windowsill. "What's with the mob of little men in pointy hats?" I asked. "My tail's not puffed out, so I don't think they're here to cause trouble. Our new stone would have kicked in otherwise."

"They showed up this morning," Dusty said. "It's annoying. I can't get close to our usual window to talk. Six of them seem to be alive. Wait here."

The moon horse trotted off. I rattled off the tail alphabet, and then went over yesterday's vocabulary with Daisy.

Dusty walked back with two tiny old men clinging to his back. They wore red pants, blue shirts, and pointed hats. Their hands were practically braided into Dusty's mane as they hung on for dear life.

"Meenhoss, this is Kitten. Kitten, this is Meenhoss and his buddy Thorn."

344

"Call me Hoss." The little fellow tipped his hat and nearly tumbled off Dusty's back, but Daisy steadied him with her nose. He went on. "I'm from a place the norms call the Adirondack Mountains."

Mountains again, yeah. Why am I not surprised?

What are norms?" I asked.

"Humans," he said. "They're causing us all kinds of trouble, especially with our Jersey Devil. Someone is trying to frame him."

"What's a Jersey Devil?" Daisy asked.

"Wait a minute," Dusty said. "Frame him for what?"

Hoss took a deep breath. "Bobby, our devil, used to be a ravenous meat eater until a mutual friend of ours, Lisa..." He pulled his hat off and leaned forward, revealing part of someone's lip prints on his bald head. "...intervened. Bobby hasn't had meat in two hundred years. He's not only vegetarian now, he's gone total vegan. Practices meditation, yoga, and tai chi. It's made a new monster out of him."

"I still don't understand." Dusty said.

"Someone has been killing local cows and sheep, trying

to stir up the locals. Not to mention free publicity for the resort that's on the nearby lake. People are flocking to us with cameras, guns, hunting dogs, you name it. A gnome can't even go for a walk in the woods without being discovered.

Bobby is so freaked out, the poor guy has gone underground until the heat dies down. Worse yet, we're afraid he might fall off the wagon. After two centuries of sobriety too, it would be a crying shame."

"What do you want us to do? How can we help him, and you?"

"We're sure you'll think of something. Word on the street is you went toe-to-toe with you-know-who and beat him. You put him in the big place, and he can't get out." The little man grinned, revealing tiny white teeth.

Dusty regarded the little man. "Meenhoss—"

"Please, that's Hoss."

"Hoss, I don't see that we can do anything for him."

Hoss's little body deflated like a balloon with a slow leak. "Between the barbeques and all the trash the norms leave behind, they're destroying our mushroom crops. It's how we get by in the winter. Mushrooms are also the secret to keep Bobby from going feral on us."

"Really?" I asked. "I'm very fond of meat too and..."

The little man grinned. "Oh, we're experimenting with Shiitake mushrooms. The secret is in the marinade..."

"Do you mind?" Daisy stomped her foot. "Back to business."

"Look, there are tourists stomping around all over the place and ruining our mushrooms. The humans prance around in shorts and t-shirts and it's making Bobby lose his willpower and concentration. With all the devil hunters around it's making him irritable and...hungry for meat. He might even turn on us too. Help us solve the frameup so people will leave us to our quiet life and Bobby can go back to his yoga and contemplation. If anyone can do it, it's you. Please?" Hoss took his hat off.

A big, horsey grin stretched across the big guy's mouth. He had that look in his eye that reminded me of the night he took on Magus to save Jangles.

"Are you kidding? We just got back," I sighed.

Hoss's buddy stepped up. "You all know what's living on this place, right? Someone told you about—"

Hoss slapped his partner with his hat. "Don't be rude.

Ain't none of our business."

"Sorry, meant no offense." The little gnome bowed.

"All right, team." Dusty pointed his face into the rising sun in a way that would have Mark taking pictures of him for Facebook. "We're off to the Adirondacks."

ABOUT THE AUTHOR

T. J. Akers wants to be a multi-millionaire when he grows up and give his wealth away to help his favorite causes—churches, schools, and animal shelters. Since the millions have been slow in coming, he's had to settle for working at a state university as a computer technician, volunteering at church and his local animal shelter. Oh, and writing stories to entertain people, especially younger readers.

His short story, *Necessary Evil*, has been published in the science fiction anthology No Revolution Too Big, (Helping Hands Press, April 2014). Another short story *Elfanticide,* appeared in the anthology Tides of Impossibility (Skipjack Press, April 2015).

He holds a Master of English degree from Minnesota State University, Mankato, and can often be found roaming the library on his breaks, especially in the children's and young adult sections.

He lives with his beloved wife of thirty years, his dog, and three cats.

ABOUT MARK, DUSTY, DAISY, AND KITTEN

Mark Peterson is a monster hunter. When he's not tracking cryptids like the Mothman or Bigfoot, he runs a gym floor refinishing business and is a published nature photographer.

From 2007 to 2010, Mark was the field producer for MonsterQuest, a series on The History Channel. The real Dusty and Daisy took him and supplies into hard to reach wilderness sites where Mark installed trail cameras, shot video of wildlife,

installed more trail cameras, filmed scenery backdrops, and scouted more potential filming sites for the series. These real-life expeditions included actual scientists and forensic specialists.

The monsters and locations Mark and Dusty encountered on these excursions form the backdrop for the Dusty stories, with just a little magic thrown in for good measure.

The real Kitten was part of a litter of feral cats born on Mark's Minnesota ranch. Dusty discovered him, just like in the book, and an instant bond formed between horse and cat.

Mark, the horses, and Kitten genuinely enjoy being with one another and most days they're all outside enjoying northern Minnesota.

Learn more about Mark, Dusty, Daisy, and Kitten at: www.DustysAdventures.com.

CPSIA information can be obtained
at www.ICGtesting.com
Printed in the USA
FFHW021050010319
50753188-56166FF